frica pulse

T0346704

THE LAWSUIT OF THE TWINS

SEK Mqhayi

Translated from isiXhosa by Thokozile Mabeqa

OXFORD
UNIVERSITY PRESS

SOUTH AFRICA

OXFORD
UNIVERSITY PRESS

Oxford University Press is a department of the University of Oxford.
It furthers the University's objective of excellence in research, scholarship,
and education by publishing worldwide. Oxford is a registered trade mark of
Oxford University Press in the UK and in certain other countries.

Published in South Africa by
Oxford University Press Southern Africa (Pty) Limited

Vasco Boulevard, Goodwood, N1 City, P O Box 12119, Cape Town,
South Africa

Ityala Lamawele was originally published in isiXhosa by Lovedale Press in 1914.

The moral rights of the translator have been asserted.

First published 2018

The Lawsuit of the Twins

ISBN 978 0 19 074439 7 (print)
ISBN 978 0 19 073419 0 (ebook)

First impression 2018

Typeset in Utopia Std 10.5pt on 15.5pt
Printed on 70gsm woodfree paper

Acknowledgements
Co-ordinator at the Centre for Multilingualism and Diversities Research, UWC: Antjie Krog
Publisher: Helga Schaberg
Project manager: Liz Sparg
Editor: Mary Reynolds
Book and cover designer: Judith Cross
Illustrator: James Berrangé
Typesetter: Aptara Inc.
Printed and bound by: Academic Press

We are grateful to the following for permission to reproduce photographs: Shutterstock/Juan
Nel/227886115 (cover); South African National Library, Cape Town (pp. xiii, 2); CMDR
(p. 83).

The authors and publisher gratefully acknowledge permission to reproduce copyright
material in this book. Every effort has been made to trace copyright holders, but if any
copyright infringements have been made, the publisher would be grateful for information
that would enable any omissions or errors to be corrected in subsequent impressions.

THIS BOOK FORMS part of a series of eight texts and a larger translation endeavour undertaken by the Centre for Multilingualism and Diversities Research (CMDR) at the University of the Western Cape (UWC). The texts translated for this series have been identified time and again by scholars of literature in southern Africa as classics in their original languages. The translators were selected for their translation experience and knowledge of a particular indigenous language. Funding was provided by the National Institute for the Humanities and Social Sciences (NIHSS) as part of their Catalytic Research Programme. The project seeks to stimulate debate by inserting neglected or previously untranslated literary texts into contemporary public spheres, providing opportunities to refigure their significance and prompting epistemic change within multidisciplinary research.

The unabridged edition of *Ityala Lamawele* consists of the story of "ityala lamawele" – the lawsuit of the twins – itself, plus various poems and pieces about Xhosa culture, history and leaders. As the focus of the Africa Pulse series is literature – fiction, poetry and drama – only the fictional story, namely that of the court case, is presented here. Some of the poems that do not occur within the story are included in the poetry anthology in this series. We acknowledge here the major work done by Professor Jeff Opland in unearthing Mqhayi's writings, especially those published in newspapers. This comprehensive and much admired translation mission at Rhodes University manifests in a series of books on isiXhosa literature also funded by the NIHSS.

Every generation translates for itself. Within the broad scope of several translation theories and the fact that every person translates differently from the next, it is hoped that this text will generate further deliberations, translations and retranslations.

Introduction

SEK Mqhayi's *Ityala Lamawele* is without doubt the best-known literary text in isiXhosa. It has not only been prescribed for literature study in schools and tertiary institutions for decades, albeit sometimes in horribly abridged versions, but has been analysed for its literary attributes in an impressive array of scholarly engagements. The problem for me with much of the scholarly engagement with Mqhayi's work is that it is preoccupied with binaries: Christianity and tradition, learnedness and un-learnedness, and contact with writing that was pioneered by Christian missionaries from the West. I want to move away from that and look at what his works can tell us about who we were before our contact with the West, and where we have been; and what we can deduce about the present from his writing, and about ourselves – even if we study these works only for their literary attributes, and only in English. The voices of Mqhayi and his contemporaries are very important at this critical time in our history when we are seeking African voices to make sense of Africa to ourselves and the rest of the world.

Mqhayi was among the earliest Xhosa authors, and he was writing soon after his people's first contact with the written word when it was brought from the West. Much of my interest in working with old texts like his lies in the specific words he and others used in their literary works. We can study the words in order to interpret the context in which the writers lived, make conjectures or assumptions about life before contact with the West, and engage with them about the present. Firstly, studying the structure and form of the words, their origins and history, and their meanings at many levels, enables us to make deductions about the users of the language, deductions which we cannot make if we study these works only in English. Secondly, as scholars engaging with concepts of the Africanisation of knowledge, we do not have a wealth of sources that we can choose to work from to draw up hypotheses about our society in terms of what we have been and why we are here now; in particular, we are short of written sources from within the African people. So these older works written in isiXhosa are immensely valuable and give us wonderful openings to both our pasts and futures. Making them available in translation in indigenous and exogenous languages opens them up for appraisal to local and global scholarship.

Mqhayi wrote the story of *The Lawsuit of the Twins* at a time when the country was volatile and violent, especially in the Eastern Cape – the oldest clashing point between black and white people in southern Africa, and the site of uprisings, wars, killings, betrayals, massacres, and starvations. Even reading some of the poetry Mqhayi wrote between 1899 and 1945 (when he died) gives one a very considered picture of what it meant to be a black person during that time in world history, especially of someone writing in that era, when the early literary greats were moulded by both indigenous ways and Christian missionary schooling.

It is interesting that in *The Lawsuit of the Twins*, Mqhayi himself says in the preface that he is writing this novella so that people understand the intricacies of African law and its similarities with Western law. He even asserts that "*Iintlanga eziMhlophe zithe zakufika kweli lizwe zafumana ukuba abantu beli lizwe baphantse baziincutshe zomthetho…baza ke nabo bacuntsula kanobom kuloo masiko nakuloo mithetho yesiXhosa*". (When the white tribes arrived in this country, they discovered that local people had a vast knowledge of law, and that they actively practised it; the whites took a lot from those traditions and Xhosa laws, absorbing them into their own laws.) So from the point of view of the law, there are many threads in this novel that lead us away from the old binary view of African and European. It challenges the epistemic ignorance of the academy and society at large; the assumption that law, justice and governability, for example, were brought to Africa from the West.

In terms of literature, for me, this novel is not just about the court case. The case is a framework that is used to illustrate how law and justice were meted out in African society in precolonial times, and the importance of social values in the rulings made during those processes. Of course the court case is also important because it shows Mqhayi's brilliance at crafting a story that draws from the oral art forms so characteristic of Xhosa society. But I read the text to see what he tells us about life in the precolonial era, and how we can make sense of that knowledge which is rooted in African and, specifically, Xhosa experience. And it is here that the text is most intriguing.

In the story the twins appeal to local authorities to determine who is to be the head of the family after the passing of their father. They first go to the headman of their area, who makes a ruling that Babini is the heir. The headman has based this on the assumption that the sequence of birth determines who the rightful heir is – as is also the case in Western society. But Wele (generally regarded as the younger twin) does not accept it, and he takes the case to the King.

Here Mqhayi's linguistic genius comes to the fore: he uses the terms *umkhuluwa*, which technically means nothing more than "elder brother", and *inkulu*, which means the eldest son in both rank and responsibility. In other words, Mqhayi splits the concept of being born first from the concept of being the rightful heir. Throughout the text Wele and the King's council make the point that one is not *umkhuluwa* by choice; it is determined by the timing of one's birth. But one's position as *inkulu* is not only achieved through the order of birth but also through behaviour and how well one performs one's required role in the position one has within one's family and wider society.

So what does this tell me about the past? A social role was not a given, it was not a right – whether you were a man or woman or leader – it came with rules and responsibilities, and you could be stripped of a predetermined role if your behaviour did not live up to your social responsibility, or if it was in conflict with it.

So Babini, the first-born of the twins, is stripped of his right as *inkulu* after his father's passing. In his ruling, the King instructs Wele, the second-born of the twins, to go and look after his father's homestead, his mother, sisters and twin brother, clearly implying that he is now *inkulu*.

The first point to make here is that this illustrates how resolutions reached in the Xhosa legal system after a dispute are not punitive, but are considerate also to the one who loses, and the purpose is to achieve some form of balance and harmony in the society as a whole. This is unlike what is typically encountered in a Western court of law, where there is always antagonism between the two sides and the resolution determines one as guilty or not guilty.

What happens? Babini returns to the home he had deserted and is cooperative. Mqhayi describes this brilliantly: "*Uthe ngqo wagoduka uBabini. Efikile ekhaya, ugqithe waya kukhangela iinkomo edlelweni; ubuye nazo kakuhle, wasuka waphothula izandla wasenga njengokungathi bekungabanga kho nto.*" (Babini walked straight home. When he arrived there, he passed the house to go and look at the cattle in the veld; he brought them to the kraal without any hitches, cleaned his hands and milked the cows, as if nothing in the world had happened.) From that day onwards, of course, he behaves for the first time as an heir is supposed to behave – proof of the corrective nature of the punishment.

The second point is that the perception we have today of our indigenous culture is that males, that is, sons and uncles, take over after a father's death and the mother is disregarded. But here the King not only orders the "new" heir, Wele, to restore the homestead to its full potential so that it can contribute to the wellbeing of the whole village but – and this is important – also to the wellbeing of the rest of the family, including the mother. We need to take note of such writings when we hypothesise about gender relations in African society. What do the practices described in the novel reveal about society's respect for its womenfolk?

Another part of the story that Mqhayi exploits to showcase Xhosa legal protocol is the account of the traditional ritual to console the twins' homestead after their father's death. The King, who must direct the proceedings during this ritual, sends the message to Wele, informing him that he will come to perform the ritual, but Wele, whom he had pronounced to be *inkulu*, tells the shocked messengers this must be wrong. Then, when the King summons the twins after the return of his messengers, Wele indicates to him that the message should be sent to the heir of his family, Babini, whose behaviour has, since the King's ruling, been characteristic of both *umkhuluwa* and *inkulu*.

Through the lawsuit, which Mqhayi skilfully uses as a framework in the novel, he challenges us to rethink the concept of heirdom, of leadership: is one a leader simply because of one's birth, or is leadership something to be earned through socially accepted behaviour, behaviour that is constructive from the smallest social unit, the family, to the largest social unit, society in general? There are five reasons why the King, after listening to testimonies from carefully chosen witnesses during the trial, announces Wele as the leader and head of his father's household: the first is the custom that a councillor always prepares the way for a chief – therefore Babini simply paved the way for Wele's leadership; the second is that Wele had received the ancestral custom of finger-cutting first; the third is that Babini forfeited his heirdom to Wele when, as a boy, he accepted a bulbul in place of his responsibility as an heir; the fourth is that Wele was circumcised first; the fifth is that he was, anyway, already the one taking care of his father's homestead. Mqhayi suggests that in matters of leadership, Xhosa society placed greater value on responsible leadership than on that predetermined on the basis of rank, in this case, birth position.

With regard to general Xhosa legal system and processes, Mqhayi makes another pertinent point: when Wele takes the case to King Hintsa, the King does not use his position to take a unilateral decision. The concept of *ukukhundla* from which the name *inkundla*, the courtyard, is derived, means "to sit in a place unswervingly for the purposes of finding solutions to problems". The King waits, he listens, he gets evidence from all possible witnesses, so that the ruling he makes is informed by deliberations that have taken place with the purpose of reaching a fair resolution to the dispute.

In contrast, the headman, Lucangwana, does not provide this opportunity. The King's *inkundla* is a space that allows everybody to participate and engage where it matters, without discriminating; it accommodates the level of detail that a legal expert trained in Western ways of collecting evidence would expect, and Mqhayi vividly makes the reader aware of it: some people passing by on oxen "interrogate" Babini and Wele; curious onlookers in the courtyard, the midwives of various ages, who are key witnesses and who affirm one anothers' testimony, the twins' sisters and mother, and the sage Khulile, whose father had once presided over a familiar case: all these provide a base from which the King can draw for the ruling he makes. They are a means "to prepare and make the way clear" for the King to give the verdict.

Mqhayi ends his preface with a passionate plea: he sees that the language of the Xhosa people and their social norms and values are fading and he charges the youth "to look carefully at precisely what will disappear when these wise and distinguished expressions and customs of their origin vanish completely". The writing of *Ityala Lamawele* is therefore a deliberate endeavour to validate the precolonial sociocultural practices of amaXhosa, using the legal system as an example. The charge above that Mqhayi makes is directed at the youth. The role of the youth in revitalising and reclaiming social values is seen throughout *Ityala Lamawele*. When the King sends out messengers to call witnesses to his Great Place, he charges them to take young people with them "to protect them from barking dogs", thereby creating spaces in which the youth are prepared for socially accepted behaviour. Mqhayi's main characters are also two young men, one of whom cannot endure the fact that the bond linking him with his twin brother is disrupted. He does everything, even gives up a potentially powerful position, so that they can work together, succeed and build a healthy homestead, a healthy village. In the end it is respect for each other and humility that results in a cohesive relationship, and not their hunger for power and authority that often defines such positions nowadays, and indeed did at the time of Mqhayi's writing.

Mqhayi cleverly uses the wise old Khulile to prophesy the coming of foreigners with their *umqulu* – meaning something voluminous, consisting of volumes, the Bible. Their coming will bring problems, volatility, poverty, great losses, but, says the sage, the solution will come from studying this very volume. Mqhayi takes a position that is neither promoting absorption into the "new", nor is it in total opposition to it, but it studies and interprets it not through the ways of others, but in its own way.

Let me return to my earlier question: what does *Ityala Lamawele* tell us about now? If we talk about decolonisation and the need to construct new knowledge that considers sources from within Africa, we have to acknowledge that a lot may have been lost, but there are a great many elements in our older texts that need to be studied and interpreted as they may well be crucial for our cultural survival. This archival material needs to be brought back to the centre and studied not only for its literary attributes, but for the insight it can give into the precolonial past, and how this can contribute to multiversality in disciplines such as law.

Professor Pamela Maseko
University of the Western Cape, Cape Town
    and Rhodes University, Grahamstown
June 2018

SEK Mqhayi (1875–1945)

Samuel Edward Krune Mqhayi is often referred to as imbongi yesizwe jikelele (the poet of the nation), and was called the "poet laureate of the African people" by the young Nelson Mandela. He was born in 1875 in Gqumashe, a village in the Eastern Cape. In his youth, he spent six years living in Centane, and the knowledge of the language and customs of the Xhosa people that he gained while living there had a great impact on his life and his future writing. He was a prolific contributor to newspapers, including the influential *Izwi Labantu*, which he also edited. He rapidly became a towering figure in isiXhosa literature. He was the first imbongi to write down his poetry, and it is said that his contribution to making new words in his novels has filled many pages in isiXhosa dictionaries. His first novel – an adaptation of the biblical story of Samson – was written in 1907, but has been lost. This was followed by *Ityala Lamawele* (The Lawsuit of the Twins) and *UDon Jadu* (Don Jadu), which have both become classics in isiXhosa literature, the former being prescribed in schools and universities to this day. Mqhayi added several stanzas to Enoch Sontonga's hymn "Nkosi Sikelel' iAfrika", now South Africa's national anthem. He also published *Imihobe Nemibongo* (Songs of Joy and Lullabies), his first published collection of poems in isiXhosa in 1927, an autobiography, *UMqhayi wase Ntab'ozuko* (Mqhayi of the Mount of Glory), in 1939 and another poetry volume, *Inzuzo* (Reward), in 1942. He twice won the May Esther Bedford Prize for Bantu literature.

Characters

Nzothwa family
Vuyisile: the late father of the twins
Wele: Babini's twin brother
Babini: Wele's twin brother
Phakiwe: a sister of the twins
Nozici: a sister of the twins
Phekesa: a paternal uncle of the twins, Lalo's older brother
"Lawule's daughter": mother of the twins, widow of Vuyisile
Lalo: a paternal uncle of the twins, Phekesa's younger brother

Lucangwana: the headman in the region where the twins live
King Hintsa: son of Khawuta and King of the Gcaleka (see historical figures p. xvi)
Fuzile: one of King Hintsa's councillors
Ndlombose: one of King Hintsa's councillors
Mxhuma Matyeni: a member of King Hintsa's household at the Great Place
Khulile: a wise elder, son of Majeke (see historical figures p. xvi)

Teyase: an elderly midwife
Yiliwe: a midwife and aunt of the twins

Nompumza: a man from Umzimkhulu in the north

Historical figures included or referred to

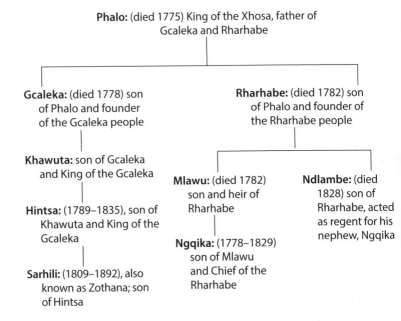

Phalo: (died 1775) King of the Xhosa, father of Gcaleka and Rharhabe

Gcaleka: (died 1778) son of Phalo and founder of the Gcaleka people

Khawuta: son of Gcaleka and King of the Gcaleka

Hintsa: (1789–1835), son of Khawuta and King of the Gcaleka

Sarhili: (1809–1892), also known as Zothana; son of Hintsa

Rharhabe: (died 1782) son of Phalo and founder of the Rharhabe people

Mlawu: (died 1782) son and heir of Rharhabe

Ngqika: (1778–1829) son of Mlawu and Chief of the Rharhabe

Ndlambe: (died 1828) son of Rharhabe, acted as regent for his nephew, Ngqika

Others:

- **Ntsikana:** (c. 1780–c.1820) a prophet and Christian evangelist
- **Nxele:** (died 1820) a war-doctor and leader of Xhosa armies
- **Majeke:** one of Phalo's councillors, and father of Khulile

The Eastern Cape of *The Lawsuit of the Twins*

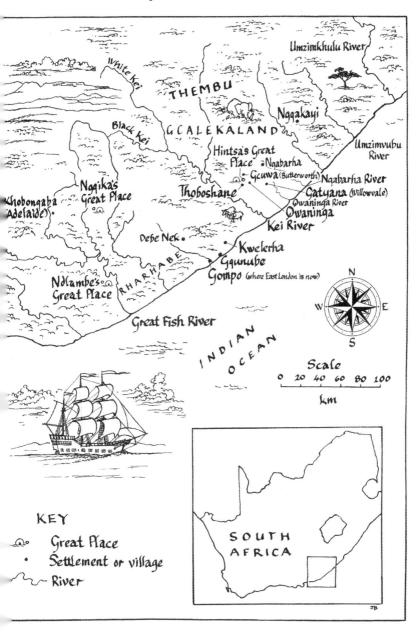

THE LAWSUIT OF THE TWINS

And it came to pass, that when she travailed,
that the one put out his hand, and the midwife took
and bound upon his hand a scarlet thread, saying,
This came out first.
And it came to pass as he drew
back his hand, that behold, his brother came out:
and she said: How has thou broken forth?
This breach be upon thee:
therefore his name was called Pharez.

Genesis, Chapter 38: 28–29 (King James Version)

SEK Mqhayi

The author of this novelette: the poet of the nation.

Where will I always be with you, as I'm just a human being –
As I'm just a person who eventually comes to visit,
As I'm just a person who eventually moves to other places,
As I'm just a person who eventually goes home.
Ncincilili! I am finished.

Preface

Although I am not an expert in law per se, I do understand that Xhosa law is not so different from that of the enlightened nations. When the white tribes arrived in this country, they discovered that local people had a vast knowledge of law, and that they actively practised it; the whites took a lot from those traditions and Xhosa laws, absorbing them into their own laws.

In this novelette I am trying to display the efforts and devotion employed by Xhosa people when tracking the law, as it has to be based on a past event, and for this I am also using a past event. I am also trying to indicate that traditionally the chief is not the sole decision-maker, as other societies tend to think.

The language and mode of life of the Xhosa people are gradually disappearing because of the Gospel and the new civilisation which came with the nations from the West, the sons of George (Gogi) and his wife (Magogi)[1].

It is up to young Xhosa males and females to look carefully at precisely what will disappear when these wise and distinguished expressions and customs of their origin vanish completely.

These are therefore deliberate endeavours to resist the wave that will demolish the whole nation. You, too, should strive to support these attempts.

I am yours in the struggle of the nation,

SE Krune Mqhayi
Mpongo
September 1914

The court

This trial was held at Gcuwa (Butterworth), at the place where the Methodist Church used by black people is currently situated, and where the Great Place once was.

The king

The presiding king was Hintsa:

> The eyebrow onlookers say he is of angry mien,
> A bull whom they praise for goring before he has gored.

Hintsa was Khawuta's son; Khawuta was born of Gcaleka, Gcaleka was born of Phalo, and Phalo was Tshiwo's son, of Ngconde, of Togu, of Sikhomo, of Ngcwangu, of Tshawe, of Nkosiyamntu, of Malangana, of Xhosa.

Contents

1

The charge

"I'm laying a charge!"

"Proceed!"

"I'm laying a charge against Babini!"

"Proceed!"

"Babini has left me hanging, handicapping me!"

"Proceed!"

"Since we are so closely related, he presumes to be the heir, and I presume to be the heir."

"Proceed!"

"Now that the head of the family is deceased, it is difficult to run the household affairs, as neither of us wishes to stand back; we both claim to be senior!"

"Proceed!"

"I have decided to bring this matter to the court here, for it to be resolved for us!"

"Proceed!"

"I've said enough and I step down, my lord!"

"Proceed – proceed! Mh—m—m! By the way! By the way! Are you saying you are laying a charge?"

"I say I'm laying a charge."

"Are you laying a charge against Babini?"

"Yes."

"Whose son is Babini?"

"He is Vuyisile's son."

"How is this person named Babini related to you?"

"He is my elder brother."

"Do you say – do you say he has left you hanging?"

"I say so."

"Why do you say that?"

"I say that because he does not allow me to attend to the matters of our home."

"Matters like what?"

"How can I explain the complexities of family matters?"

"I am asking, in which affairs has Babini left you hanging?"

"I said from the beginning that Babini was waiting for me to take the lead; and I, from my side, waited for Babini to take the lead. We became two bulls in one kraal. For things to go well, this is something that cannot be."

"So, then: out with it."

"Do you not hear me?"

"Make it clear."

"This is what it is."

"You have not laid a charge yet; you keep on avoiding the issue, talking in riddles, just telling stories – telling stories," Ntentema said, leaving in a huff.

"What are you saying, young man?" asked Fuzile, a man of the Ngqosini clan who was lying nearby, listening. "You say you're laying a charge against Babini?"

"I say I'm laying a charge against Babini."

"You say Babini is your elder brother?"

"That is what I was saying, Your Honour."

"What are you now saying?"

"I am still saying that, Your Honour."

"Who is laying the claim, you or your brother?"

"It is he."

"Do you say he is the one claiming heirdom?"

"I say so."

"What about your statement that he is your *elder* brother?"

"That is the word from the people, not mine."

"What are you saying, young man? What are you saying? Where are those people now?"

"That is exactly what I came for, to this court, so that it can be solved for us, because this Babini and I saw the sun on the same day."

"How?"

"By being twins."

"O-h! Mh-m-m! Are you one of a twin?"

"We are twins."

"Which one was born first?"

"It's Babini."

"It's Babini?"

"It's Babini."

"Does his name mean the twoness of being twins?"

"It's exactly so."

"Then what is your name?"

"I am Wele."

"Whose sons are you?"

"We are the sons of Vuyisile."

"From where?"

"From Thoboshane."

"Of which clan?"

"Of the Nzothwa clan."

"Under whose jurisdiction?"

"Under L…"

As the plaintiff was speaking, Kosani of the Vala clan and Dlisa of the Gorha clan came past on galloping oxen, asking: "Tell us! Why are you here at the Great Place?"

"M-m, I am a plaintiff."

"What is your complaint?"

"I am laying a charge against Babini."

"Yes?"

"He says Vuyisile's household is rightfully his."

"Yes?"

But by this time Dlisa and Kosani were already disappearing, because they never really intended to stop properly.

"Just say, young man," continued Fuzile, "under whose jurisdiction?"

"Under Lucangwana's."

"What did Lucangwana say when you took the matter to him?"

"This is the third month of isiLimela[2], my lord..., my lord, that I have raised this matter with Lucangwana."

"And what does Lucangwana say?"

"My lord, Lucangwana says I am just playing, because no last-born has ever dictated the affairs of the homestead while the heir is still alive."

"And who is the heir?"

"It's Babini."

"Does Lucangwana say that?"

"Lucangwana says that."

Earlier, Qavile, a rich man of the Mvulane clan, had arrived at the Great Place with a group of men. After the plaintiff, Wele, had explained his complaint, they bombarded him with questions. However, when they heard Lucangwana's verdict, they paused.

Lucangwana's ruling was discussed intensely in front of the King, with all twenty of his councillors, including Fuzile and Gqomo, a wise old man of the Bamba clan. When they stepped down, Wisizwi, of the Tshonyane clan, a great orator in the Khawuta court[3], was heard saying, "I have now heard what I've never heard before!" He emptied his pipe. Mancapha of the Qocwa clan, quite a senior there, added, "I have lived and lived on this earth, until I finally tasted its bile." He took out the last tobacco leaves that he had put in his pocket the previous night.

Mkrweqana, a very wide-awake person, who was often present at the Great Place and was also given tasks to do there, said, "But now it's our time; we're going to fix things." He spoke while softening the leather thong that he was preparing for a dance later at Siko's place at Ngxangxasini. He was angrily glared at by Rholoma of the Cethe clan, a senior man, who was carving an ebony stick. The King, constantly smoking, looking down, listening, did not say a word.

By this time, Wele had left. He was told to go home. His case was to be considered.

2

The hearing of the case

After the dance at Siko's place, King Hintsa sent Qavile and Mdunywa, two young and promising men of the Tipha clan, to call the headman Lucangwana to the Great Place. He sent them late so that they could sleep over and have the opportunity to deliberate matters concerning the case before their return the next morning.

Since Lucangwana had already heard the case, it did not seem likely that he would be happy about this; and he was not the kind of headman who spoke privately, behind the scenes, with councillors around issues related to a court case.

On their way to Lucangwana, Qavile and Mdunywa walked past the home of Nqwakuza of the Nyele clan. There they found a group of men relishing the last of a dish of cow's feet. The animals had died of a disease that affects calves. The two men greeted the group, and the group echoed their greeting. The two knelt down, asking a boy for an ember to light their pipes. The men teased them a lot after this festive meal, claiming that they had missed everything, arriving so late on their ageing baboons.

Whilst they were still smoking their pipes, they were asked where they were from, and what their destination was. As they had come from the Royal House, the local men were keen to know how far the case of Vuyisile's younger son had got. The two men denied having any knowledge of it. So what was it all about?

Nqwakuza explained: "Nowadays, when the young men become rich, they like to go to court for trivialities. There is a young man there who, for three years, has been bothering us, claiming to be the heir, whereas, he was born last. There's a rumour that the case has already been taken to the Royal House; we thought we could hear from you what was happening."

The messengers got up, shook their blankets out and left. It was dusk when they arrived at the home of the headman, Lucangwana. Because it was known where they had come from, good care was taken of them. After they had shared some news, the young men interrogated the headman assiduously, so he revealed all the particulars of the case to them. He had already suspected that it was the reason for being summoned to the Royal House. He detailed everything to them, and, in turn, asked them about any developments concerning the case.

The next day, in the late morning when the cows had been milked, the men left after Lucangwana had told them to inform the Royal House that he was coming; he would arrive at dusk. And at dusk Lucangwana indeed arrived, accompanied by Madume, who was another wise older man of the Hegebe clan, and a young man, Sigadi, to protect them from barking dogs. The King instructed that they be accommodated at the Royal House. They slept there with Ngqokoma of the Mpemvu clan and Malinga of the Ngwevu clan. These men were known for their loyalty in keeping Royal House secrets.

At dawn, men from Thoboshane, where the plaintiff and accused hailed from, also departed from home, without any of them really knowing why they had been called. Men were ordered to tell everybody that there would be a meeting at the Royal House on the third day.

Then on the third day, from dawn to sunset, councillors from all directions gathered. By the late morning, when the cows were returning for the morning milking, the Royal House was filled with people in red ochre-dyed[4] attire. Wele was waiting attentively with his maternal uncle, Mgqaliso, of the Mpandle clan. Babini and his two fathers[5] had also arrived, and settled in another part of the court. Right through the morning, the King remained inside the Royal House; however, after some time his son appeared, bearing the skin of an eland, and spread it in the centre between the councillors. When he had laid it out neatly, the master, the chief came, with a sombre and serious expression on his face. The whole court greeted this representative of the King with his praise-name, "A! Hail! Zanzolo!" The big man did not respond, just sat down on his seat covered with the eland skin. Not long after he had sat down, he quietly sent a message to Mbali, the hero of the Mpinga clan, asking why the whole morning was being squandered. Mbali did not waste a minute further and signalled to Wele, the plaintiff, to lay his complaint before the court. Wele explained, and explained, and explained, and then stopped, but then continued using that very expression: "I explained."

Thereafter Babini was asked to give his version. He proceeded as follows: "Your lordships and gentlemen, I know nothing, because I've also been just summoned. The little I know is that I was conceived by a woman of the Mpandla clan and fathered by Vuyisile. I am a twin, together with my younger brother who is suing me today. The midwives who attended my mother during her delivery say I'm the one who saw the light first; Wele came last. As we grew up, we grew up accepting it like that. During circumcision, we were circumcised without anything repudiating what we knew. Till we were left by our deceased father, Vuyisile, there was no difference of opinion anywhere. It's only now that I hear I should step aside for Wele so that he can handle the matters of Vuyisile's family because he is the heir; and this is said by him with his own mouth." The men burst out laughing.

Babini continued: "I have often been summoned by Lucangwana, who told me they are discussing this matter; they discussed and discussed it, and found that the matter has no solution; and I get sent home with the matter still hanging. What I'm saying, honourable men, is that the one who has something to present to you, is the one who should be heard; I therefore stop."

Mbali turned to the court and said, "So say the twins, councillors." Mxhuma of the Khomanzi-Qhinebe clan spoke first, addressing the plaintiff, Wele: "Did you say you are complaining because you have not been given the position of heir?"

"Yes, Your Honour."

"Are you familiar with the fact that you came after Babini, although you were born on the same day?"

"Yes, Your Honour."

"Do you know that it is tradition that the one who comes first becomes the heir here in Tshiwo's[6] kingdom?"

"Yes, Your Honour."

"Are you coming here, young man, to ask what the law should do for you?" Wele remained quiet and did not answer.

Mxhuma continued: "So then, Vuyisile's son, you come here to ask the court to do *what* exactly for you?" Wele kept quiet and said nothing.

Mxhuma proceeded. This time he turned to Babini and said, "Do this for the court, Vuyisile's son, help Khawuta's people. This is the first time something like this has been heard in the Gcaleka house. Therefore, the matter must be heard so that its gist can be understood and unravelled, including its bitterness. You are saying that you and Wele were born of the same woman, on the same day."

"That's what I say, sir."

"Did you grow up together and get circumcised together?"

"Yes, sir."

"When you were growing up, did you ever talk about this matter?"

"Which one, sir?"

"The matter of being twins."

"Yes, sir, we often talked about it; and the other boys frequently referred to me being so small, and my younger brother being so big, having a beard, and I being so smooth and younger looking."

"They were saying that! What were those boys suggesting?"

"No, Your Honour, the boys, being childish, were saying we must change places: I to be the younger one, and Wele with the beard to be the heir."

"H-e-e! And then did you ever do that?"

"Do what, Your Honour?"

"Change places."

"I cannot say."

"Spell it out clearly, young man, make it clear."

"We are not talking about young boys' foolishness here, sir."

"Yes, I'm not saying you should talk about that; I have asked you to clarify this point: have you ever been so foolish as to exchange places?"

At this moment, Siphendu of the Zangwa clan arrived and asked, "What's this? When is this case going to be heard? Why is the court wasting time with boy-trivialities?"

"Easy, take it easy, Siphendu, the court is still in session," said Gqomo. Siphendu wanted to force his will, but was cautioned by other men to back down.

Mxhuma persisted: "I'm still waiting, my son. Clarify this matter: did you ever play a game, changing places with your younger brother?"

"Yes, there was something like that."

"Tell us!"

"One day we went bird hunting, we were a team of boys; some came back with prey, and I came back empty-handed, so some of the boys suggested I should be given some by Wele. Without hesitation, Wele said, only on condition that seniority would be his. Some of the boys forced me and after I swore that Wele could be the elder, I was then given a bird, a sombre bulbul."

"There he says it, honourable men," Mxhuma said, and covered himself with the leopard skin he had received from the Great Place on the day he brought the eland skin. After this, the people sat silently in the courtyard until Mancapha was heard saying, "This will have its own consequences." He took out a tinder-box, struck a match, and smoked. "Lucangwana treated this case superficially; today these men of the chief's kraal are delving deep," said Mganu, the elder, shaking out his blankets, and then he sat down next to the kraal.

At this point a man of the Ntakwenda clan, Ndlombose, said, "Be merciful, honourable men, let there be mercy, let there not be anger, let there not be a case. These fighting children are ours. The father is no more, he is dead, he died amongst us; this has never happened before; these children are ours, the peacemakers are us. Let us narrate the events, let us go back, let us rectify matters." Then Ndlombose covered himself.

Maduma, from Lucangwana's area, turned to Wele. "Are you claiming the heirship since that day of the bulbul?"

"Those are the fruits and assurances of the heirdom that I possess anyway, since my birth."

"No, young man, don't speak like that. Birth tells you your place. Is Babini the last born? What is it that tells you which is which?" The young man was quiet. At this moment there was only silence.

Then Zwini came up. "Who was the midwife the day you were born?"

"She was grandmother Teyase, and an aunt from my father's side, Yiliwe."

Mxhuma suddenly got up. "Did the homestead have the ceremony to comfort the bereaved[7]? How was it comforted?"

At this point it was decided to summon the midwives, Teyase and Yiliwe.

3

The testimony of the midwives

When the midwives arrived, Daliwe of the Hegebe clan, a Thembu man, questioned them. He asked Teyase if she was the one who had helped Vuyisile's wife to deliver the twins. She confirmed it, and thereafter all the questions were answered by her and confirmed by Yiliwe who was with her during that birth. They recounted that Vuyisile's wife had tended to have difficulty in giving birth, and even the people of her family who were there to help her had lost patience and left. Her pregnancy had been extremely difficult, and had already lasted for ten months.

"Early on the morning of the second day, a Tuesday, this woman felt labour pains," said Teyase. "By sunrise, the baby had put out his hand, and it was clear that things were now happening. The summer's day turned towards sunset, and the baby's hand was still showing. At that point Zwini appeared and said, 'Don't let me interrupt you! By the way, by the way, there's talk that this woman may give birth to twins.'"

"Yes," Teyase continued, "this woman had been in the pains of labour for longer than we expected. And the length of her pregnancy had led us to approach amagqirha, diviners, about her belly. They said that there was nothing wrong with the woman's belly, but that there were two children inside it, and they were alive. They said she'd give birth when the time for that came. Another diviner even said that the twins were boys."

Then Daliwe said, "Eh-eh! We're still listening, you know."

Teyase continued and said, "When sunset approached and this hand was still showing, I became worried, and eventually I found a sharp blade and cut off the top joint of the little finger. Just when I'd finished that, the little hand went back into the mother again. This woman's labour pains made us uncomfortable right through to sunset that day. Night fell, then morning broke. At sunrise on the third day, Wednesday, the twin that we claim to be the eldest appeared."

"Babini, that is?" asked Mxhuma.

"Yes, this Babini. We looked for the finger with the missing joint, but no, it was not there."

"Was it just you and Yiliwe there?"

"No, the team of women was present already. I did not sleep alone that night as Yiliwe was still a child. The issue of ingqithi, this cutting of the last joint of the finger, is known by others, for whom I had done it when they had given birth; but this amused them, and they said it must be the Nzothwa clan's custom to do the ingqithi cut before one is born. To this day there are women who remember that day, and who know about it. Why they were not summoned, I don't know; that is not my place to ask.

"All the women who were there knew about this issue of ingqithi; anyone who came was told that the reason for the hand being pulled back in was because it had been cut. As Babini was being born, all of us were looking for the cut finger, ingqithi, together."

Teyase continued, "It happened during the late morning, when the cows were leaving the kraal, after they had been milked, that the second twin was born, the one we claim is the last born."

"Is it the plaintiff in front of us?"

"Yes, this Wele who is in front of us now. Indeed he came out with this small amputation."

"What did the women say about this matter?"

"Say what about what, about their happiness that the woman had given birth?"

"No, I mean about the twins, which twin is the eldest; or did they just leave it?"

"No, there had been such a difference of opinion, others saying this is the elder one, others saying that is the elder."

"Did they come to a conclusion?"

"No, I reprimanded them, questioning them as to what they were trying to do, making my child's children argue before the day arrived that they could argue for themselves; what evil were they predicting?"

"Is that all?"

"Yes, as far my knowledge goes."

Daliwe then addressed Yiliwe, asking if she could support the things said by her mother. Yiliwe confirmed that she could. Teyase was asked which other adult woman had been present during the delivery. She named Singiswa who was then also summoned. When she was asked about what she remembered about the time of the twins' birth, she repeated exactly what Teyase had told them to the very end. Then the women were asked to leave.

4

The case is referred to adjudicators

Now the ears of the men seemed to open. Murmurs were heard among them; some were saying that Wele was the elder, while others were saying that the issue of the cutting off of the finger joint meant nothing. When it grew calm again, Xolilizwe of the Jwarha clan stood up and said, "There is still Mxhuma's question: did this homestead have the ceremony to comfort the bereaved?"

It became very quiet at this moment, and the men grew serious and thoughtful. Then Magqaza, of the Khwemte clan, remembered: "There was this death, then, of a councillor, that was traced back to a battle during the Mfecane." This settled the issue quickly: due to the turmoil during those times, and despite the fact that Vuyisile's death had been reported to the Great Place, the homestead had never had the comforting ceremony.

Now the chief asked Wele what had made him bring this case before the law. Wele answered, "I'm concerned about not seeing eye to eye with my father's child, my brother Babini; and because of that, affairs at our homestead have become confusing and stagnant. Therefore I've decided to bring this matter to our home here, so that it can be resolved for us."

The chief: "Did you ever mention this to Babini, and remind him about the day of the bulbul, and show him the missing fingertip that you got before he was born?"

Wele: "I tried all of this, Your Honour, but it didn't help; that was what drove me initially to the place of the headman, Lucangwana, but there I did not get any clarity."

The chief: "Why don't you accept Lucangwana's verdict, my son?"

Wele: "As I understand it, Your Honour, the matter's like this. You, Your Honour, are not the one to clear the way for the councillor; it's the councillor who clears the way for you. Why is it that when my councillor clears the way for me, there is an argument? I have shown my hand to prove that I received the tradition first. So why is it so problematic here within the law, Your Honour? The day we were circumcised, I was circumcised first, to indicate that I'm the heir."

Lucangwana conferred with Babini regarding the circumcision. Babini confirmed it but said that the guardians had made a mistake in circumcising Wele first. "So what's this?" exclaimed Lucangwana, covering himself again with the blanket of animal skins. The councillors kept pulling and pushing each other, saying, "You, ask now." "It's your turn," until no one had any questions left. Then Ndlombose said, "The real decisive moment is this one, honourable men. This is the time that needs elders. Between these children, we don't want to wrong either one of them; they are ours, we have given birth to them – we have given birth to them – we have given birth to them."

At sunset, all the people were allowed to go back to their homes, to return the next morning. The highly esteemed stayed for the night at the Great Place where the issue of these two young men was then to be extensively discussed. The discussion was mainly based on Ndlombose's word that this case needed very wise old men as it was perhaps an issue with a precedent. After the discussions, it was decided that they would send some men to Nqabarha, to the Majeke home, to fetch Khulile of the Qwambi clan, and bring him to the Great Place.

The councillors thought of Khulile because his father, Majeke, had also been a sage and had saved the Great Place when it had a problem; that was in the year that the tradition of the Right-hand House was established, in the time of Phalo[8]. Back then, long ago, Majeke had been fetched from Nqabarha, although by that time his eyes were blind from age.

The next morning, people descended like locusts on the Great Place. The court became fuller and fuller, and it was red with people's ochre-dyed attire and the red ochre on women's faces; each and every one seemingly wanted to hear the verdict with their own ears when it was presented, because the case was on everybody's lips in every small homestead.

In the morning when the sun was high and it was becoming hot, the young men appeared with the King's animal skin, and then he followed. The people in the courtyard were heard exclaiming "A! Hail! Zanzolo!" The King responded with dignity, and sat down. Mbali began by recharging people's interest, asking them to remember where they had left off yesterday.

Sonti then summarised the previous day's discussion. Sonti was Mxhuma's younger brother; they were Matyeni's sons, of the Qhinebe clan. When Sonti was finished, the plaintiff and accused were asked where Vuyisile had died. Both of them agreed that their father had died at Luvulweni, during an attack in a battle of the Mfecane. After some additional questions were posed by the honourable men, not much more seemed to be done that day, except that the issue concerning Majeke was discussed at the house, when it was now raised by Mxhuma, Matyeni's son.

"As you know, House of Khawuta," Mxhuma said, "the matters of this house are not taken lightly. They are thoroughly investigated until the roots have been exposed, and then dug up. Only if the root fails us do we resort to wandering about the veld. Vuyisile's sons have awakened us to something that we have overlooked, and they have alerted our Great Place to the need to investigate how we can solve it."

Mbali then continued speaking about these homesteads, and he spoke about the old sage, Majeke, who was well remembered here at Phalo's Great Place, although he himself was no more, and his sons were now the elders.

Three men were asked to go to Nqabarha to Majeke's homestead – Malinga Xhego of the Nzothwa clan; Mxhuma Matyeni of the Qhinebe clan; and Lucangwana Nyathi of the Khwemnte clan. Riding-oxen were prepared for them, and they were to be accompanied by two young men, Sigadi and Vukubi.

By now, it was already the time of the full moon. People attending the trial were told to wait until they were called at the following new moon. The period was also extended so that Khulile would have time to rest, and also to think about the matter, as it was widely known that he was quite an old man.

When the people started dispersing to go home, Bhukwana, son of Langeni of the Ntakwenda clan (Ndlombose's younger brother), who was a poet, although not a poet of the Great Place, began to recite:

It's the first time I witness a never-ending trial!
It's the first time I witness a never-ending trial!
Day in, day out we hurry; day in, day out we put on shoes.
How many bulls now in the homestead of Phalo?
We used to say there was none other than Hintsa.
We used to say that the ferocious animal of Nobutho is the
    only bull –
The bull that climbs on the backs of other bulls.
I became so ashamed when I heard that it has castrated itself
And brought itself to Nqabarha, to Majeke's place.
Is this bull not potent?

Back home, families are dying, burning each other
For a little matter that came up through women,
Teyase and Singiswa, concerning past events.
Make the bull show its potency while there is still time.
Nothing will come out of Nqabarha.

When this man started reciting, nobody left; everybody just stood where they were, listening.

Then, while people were still feeding their ears, pandemonium broke out in the centre of a group of dancing men. It was Ndlombose. He suddenly began to fight viciously with his younger brother because of something that he had said, and he was already grasping a short spear. But some of the men intervened, one saying: "Why is it that when Vuyisile's sons are fighting, there are stupid people standing on the mountain rejoicing? By my sister's name, where does such a thing belong?" Bhukwana apologised to his older brother, Ndlombose, and everybody went home.

5

The messengers at Nqabarha

The messengers departed, leaving the Great Place. The weather was good; cicadas sang, and the grass warblers were fluttering their wings; longclaws[9] flew in front of the men, calling upon the ancestors, giving praises to their journey and asking for it to be blessed. Wild animals were waking up, and they stood along the path simply looking at them, doing them no harm.

On the first night the messengers slept at Qwaninga, at the homestead of a chief's son who ruled over a large area. They were welcomed with open arms and an animal was slaughtered. The reason for their journey had preceded them, so they were asked about the latest developments. However, the messengers divulged nothing, saying that the time had not yet come to discuss anything. The people at Qwaninga told them that the majority of men stood by Lucangwana's verdict.

The messengers stayed for two days, then left and arrived at dusk – the time when hares run around – at the Majeke homestead at Nqabarha. They were given a hut to sleep in, and were shown the respect they deserved, and were not asked for any news until the second day.

When they introduced themselves, Khulile, son of the late Majeke, not only knew them all, but also who their fathers and forefathers were. Because the old man, Khulile, was at ease and relaxed, his old age was not visible to anybody: he was handsome, looked strong, and was able to hear and see well. The one who had aged was his younger brother, Gebenga.

On the third day at noon, the Majeke family at last gathered with those of their sons and grandchildren, who were mature men already, to ask for news from the Great Place. Thanguthangu, Khulile Majeke's only son, did the questioning. Mxhuma Matyeni from the Great Place explained what was happening while his colleagues verified, added and corrected the facts as he continued until they had finished.

A few questions were put, and then they stopped. The Majeke men were asking: as the objections in this matter were one-sided, what could be the problem? But they were also saying to themselves: these days, people think that a person is born twice, but a person is born only once: the person who is born in childhood, is the one in maturity and the one in old age.

The men from the Great Place were asked if they would mind if the issue they had come for could also be conveyed to the household of the chief's son who was in charge of this area. The messengers agreed, saying that what was wanted at home was to get to the core truth of the matter; talking about it in calm places like these could be exactly the way to come up with the truth.

By this time there was a whole commotion among the people of that area. Some men felt themselves directly affected by the case and rushed to the Majeke homestead. The lawsuit of the twins had created anxiety even among those who were not twins, and it was already heatedly debated on all sides.

Some of the people of the area brought cattle to be slaughtered for the councillors from the Great Place to eat while they were there. They felt obliged to do so, not that Khulile did not have food for the men, but because, truly, the Majekes did not have very much livestock. The elders there were enjoying themselves;

they spoke with enthusiasm, and voiced their opinions on the lawsuit. Finally, the chief's son called an imbizo, at which he told the people that Khulile had been summoned by the Great Place to advise on certain aspects of the case. Nobody responded; they merely listened and then one could hear the echoing of gratitude as the house unanimously agreed that he should go; that it was fine. At this point there was singing and dancing, and after the slaughtering, the upper quarter-leg up to the breast was given to the men from the Great Place so that they had meat in abundance.

In the mean time, while the messengers were away, the court case of the twins continued. This one said this, that one said that, others were judging the whole case from the hills, and some wanted to know what was expected from the Majeke family. Was he, Khulile, now suddenly in the place of Hintsa, the King, son of Khawuta? Vuyisile's daughters, too, were making their own noise: the older sister, born before the twins, and the younger one, praised Wele as a person who looked after the people of their father's house, who had a caring hand for the girls and visitors at the homestead, and was the one who took care of the livestock of the whole household. According to them, Babini was dancing for the whole nation, chasing far-away ceremonies and always carrying his dance attire.

The middle sister, born after the twins, praised Babini: "As he is the elder twin, he is the elder; even Khulile will not change Lucangwana's verdict. Everybody knows there are many loiterers who are still the heirs at their homes. What is it for, then, that my father's child is so interrogated, and important rivers are crossed for him?"

At the Royal House, when the men talked among themselves, and when they reached the issue of the instrument used for circumcision, they usually just judged with their hearts, and nothing was said verbally. But when they reached Wele's utterance, that it was the chief who should have his way cleared by the councillors, they could not arrive at any truth at all. Things remained like that at home while the messengers who had been sent to Nqabarha were away.

On the tenth day the messengers at Nqabarha became anxious, saying that it had been days since they left home, and they did not know what was happening back there at the Great Place. So the questioning stopped, and they were allowed to leave the following day from this place where they had been chatting with the men and the chief, telling stories that everybody found exciting. People were sorry when the news came that the men from the Great Place were leaving Nqabarha the next day.

Initially Khulile wanted to send his speech through the messengers, but the men refused. In the morning the men from the Royal House armed themselves, harnessed their riding-oxen well, and filled their water bottles made of skin. Khulile left with Makhunzi (the son of his younger brother, Gebenga) and they were given a young man from the Royal House, namely Gqarhi, to accompany them.

When they left, a crowd of people came to say goodbye, and Ngaye, Zekela's son was heard reciting:

Go Majeke's son, and come back well!
Your father was fetched some years ago, and there was no disgrace,
You are his son, be without shame.
Your riding-ox is beautiful; it has not disgraced those of the Great Place.
I say, go Majeke's son, we give permission,

The knotty whip with off-shoots, from the house of Tokazi,
The bull that partners with those of the Great Place to produce
    cows with milk,
I like it that those of my home are not forsaken to become good
    for nothing.
Go and enter that household, it is your own home;
Your age-mates left you long ago,
That's why you are a skin-vessel being emptied of its last drop;
That's why we come to you for the origin of the nation.
Go with the spirit of your home,
Go with Qamata, the God of your nation. There I leave it.

The men left as if they did not hear. They slept at Qwaninga. When people came out to see the men of the Great Place, it was as if they had been called by the blowing of ixilongo, the trumpet made from a kudu horn. People appeared in the blink of an eye, and within minutes there was a large crowd. An ox was slaughtered, and they ate meat the whole night. All the men were happy, singing and clapping hands and dancing through the night. When the night was advanced, the men from the Royal House stole away to sleep in a house allocated to them. The locals stayed for the whole night; even when dawn broke, they were still there.

In the morning the people from Qwaninga did not want the men from the Great Place to leave. Stories were started there in the courtyard, and dishes stood in a row; there was plenty of food produced in this region. The men from the Great Place were interrogated about new developments, about nations that still had cattle, about oxen that were racers, as well as on advice for reprimanding women and children.

The following day, the men from the Great Place left with Khulile. On their way, they met people asking where they were coming from, but the majority already knew without asking, because the whole nation was aware of the twins' lawsuit. They reached the Great Place at dusk; happy, well and refreshed by the journey.

6

Khulile at the Great Place

When they arrived, the messengers and the old men of Nqabarha stayed together in the same house. Several dishes were taken to them because it was assumed that they were hungry after the journey. During the night some of the prominent men went to see them, until Mxhuma pointed out that the old men were drowsy, as they had not slept since they had left Nqabarha; Mxhuma and other men of the household then had a warm and sociable evening.

The following day dawned, and again, it was as if people were called by a trumpeting horn to the Great Place; although it was not an imbizo yet, everybody wanted to see the greyhead sage, Khulile of Nqabarha. At midday, it was already red with the crowds of people at the Great Place – not really a strange occurrence, since it was usual for this place.

Khulile, whom everybody came to see, was easy to get on with, spoke well, and knew people; he was also a singer and a poet, as well as a herbalist. He was not a diviner though, revealing or giving evidence with bones and so forth. Those were the qualities Khulile came with, and it amazed people, as they had expected an aged man, blind and deaf, sedentary, just sleeping and dreaming.

Young women wanted to entertain these men from Nqabarha, but they were not given permission to do so. People from the Royal House wanted to know how old Khulile was. There were many from the generation of Khawuta (Hintsa's father) among the people there, and, when they reflected on it, they worked out that Khulile was of a generation before Khawuta, because he said that he had gone to the initiation school with Phalo – which indicated that a hundred and ten years had passed since his initiation.

Khulile was at the Great Place for three days without any meeting being called, but a group of men immediately informed him thoroughly about the court case, and the King also spoke to him.

On the fourth day, at exactly the prescribed time of the new moon, young men of the Great Place were sent to call the people to be present, asking them to share this call until it had spread through the whole nation. And so it happened, because everybody wanted to hear the outcome.

Indeed, already by the second day, people had been interacting in great numbers at the Great Place, as if the event was a ceremony, those coming from afar arriving with their riding-oxen loaded with skin bags. When the sun rose that day, there was no one absent – the place was red with their ochre-dyed clothing. All the same, the men were not happy and did not make eye contact, and the praise poets were silent. The dominant activity was smoking; the smoke of tobacco was as heavy as if something was burning.

That morning, on the fourth day, the King was already present; evidently the trial had to proceed. The issues were repeated; both twins were again asked questions and were interrogated.

The plaintiff, Wele, claimed to be the heir on the following grounds: the first one being that the way for a chief should be prepared by a councillor; the second one being that he had received the ancestral custom of finger-cutting first; the third one being that he had bought his heirdom with a bulbul when he was a boy; the fourth being that he was circumcised first on the day they were circumcised; the fifth being that he was, anyway, already the one looking after his father's homestead and organising everything about it.

The accused said that his brother was talking rubbish and petty trivialities; he was the heir, because of the simple fact that he was born first, and this was the custom: the first-born was the heir.

When the girls of their homestead were called, they testified as to who provided for them. Their mother was present and was also asked questions. Phakiwe, the girl who previously had always praised Babini, was asking why her brother was being interrogated; she now sang the same tune as the other sisters, saying that the plaintiff was the one looking after them, because Babini "has nothing, but he does not deny us what he has".

The plaintiff was asked about the charges: what did Babini do that upset the routine of things at home? The plaintiff counted three cows that had been sent out to different people without anyone knowing the reason. He talked about how Babini had refused to pay his specific share for his sister Nozici's traditional transition ceremony, which a girl undergoes at puberty, when she is initiated into young womanhood. He described how, after his father died, Babini had chased away the uncles who came to cleanse the household[10], and was chasing them away to this day.

His mother confirmed all these facts. Babini, the defendant, also confirmed them; but although he agreed indirectly, he tried to shield himself at the same time. When the questions were directed to the other two sisters, they revealed everything, yes, even the pipe cleaner and the pipe stem.

Then the defendant and plaintiff were asked to excuse themselves from the proceedings. This they did, and waited some distance away.

7

The wise old man's experiences

Now the court turned to Khulile, the wise old man of Nqabarha, saying, "So you see, Majeke's son, this is the problem that we called you for from Nqabarha. You are here with us; you see, you hear for yourself, you no longer have to listen to what we tell you. This case is the first of its kind in our generation, which is why the court thought of you. We do not have a place to hold onto and to stand on, because everything is to be decided along the lines of other cases, by comparisons, as you know. So here it is!"

After this it was quiet for a moment. When he finally stood up, Khulile had this to say: "Honourable men and everybody!" When Khulile said that, the men took their pipes from their mouths in haste, and there was absolute silence. "I do not know why you thought of me. Yes, my father, Majeke, saved his nation's home at the time of Phalo, but then, at that time, things were in order, lands were not ruined.

"What do I know? Who am I? The issue of these boys of my child, Vuyisile: I, too, will not resolve it as such, although I am a sage. Twins are people born on the same day. Here among we Xhosa people, when we resolve the issue of those born on the same day, the one born first is considered to be older.

"That issue is already entrenched without anyone having to suggest it, it is as if it's a regulation, that whoever is born first is the heir. But, through my life, and with these days here still flickering before my eyes, I have seen this contradicted successfully in other twins.

"Twins are born with a type of understanding that appears right from their birth. Their brains are sharper than those of other people; twins will predict something before it actually happens, and then it will indeed happen. Because of the way twins are, there is hardly any discussion about them of the kind that I have seen here today.

"Another thing is that they always have such an exceptional closeness between them, always agreeing with each other so that neither father nor law can come between them. That means that no one dares to interfere with anything pertaining to them, as they are one person.

"Today you have called me to solve something concerning people of this kind. Are sages more knowledgeable than you in issues pertaining to twins? Nkosiyamntu was the twin of his older brother, he was the younger twin; but he had seniority, and he took it while his elder brother, Liwana, was alive, because Liwana sold his position for a fillet of meat. The sages said Nkosiyamntu should take it, and that Liwana had bartered it away. They were basing their verdict on previous events, on precedents.

"I say this, honourable men, and then I stop. When an heir is summoned to oversee the household, it is because he has more experience, being the oldest among his siblings; there are people who are related to them whom he has known for longer; he has a lot of information that he has heard which others have not yet heard. So how is the right to be heir settled between twins, as they were born on the same day?

"Is it not actions that now must determine seniority, because even a first-born or heir loses his position if he proves to be a child by his actions? I leave the matter unclear and clumsy like that, so that you find for yourselves what you want."

Khulile sat down. It became quiet again after this, until Lucangwana stood up and spoke. "The sage of Nqabarha has spoken, honourable ones. There must not be silence, there must be answers, today there must be an outcome; details of this case have long been standing."

Ndlombose said that all that had been needed up to this time was the story; now the story had been concluded. Other councillors asked Khulile some further questions, and he answered them skilfully, assisted by Makhunzi, the son of his younger brother.

Then all the councillors of the Great Place were seen going out to talk privately, and their murmuring was heard. Here Vuyisile's cattle were talked about; no one knew where they had gone. Vuyisile's daughters were also mentioned, and the cutting of the finger-joint, and the circumcision; and the giving of the bulbul and other acts, and Nkosiyamntu. Some in the discussion group asked, "Is today the day when seniority is handed to the younger twin, or what?" One of them answered, "Never! The issue of the twins is still intact in its place. This court does not reverse Lucangwana's verdict."

8

The verdict

At this point the court asked the young men to call the plaintiff and accused, who came without delay. They took up other positions near the places they had initially occupied. The sun was scorching down. The men were sweating heavily, having lowered their blankets, looking down at the ground, nobody talking.

There were also many women at the Great Place, sitting near the kraal, talking softly. There was no wind. It was calm and quiet.

The grass warblers were fluttering their wings over the grass-veld,
The high sound of cicadas echoed through the red grass.

On this day Khawuta's son, Hintsa, stood up, a solidly built king with a very prominent forehead and hair that receded to the temples. He was a tall man, full-lipped, hairy but not too much, whose voice was clear when speaking – neither loud nor too quiet. He was a man of few words, not very humorous, but feared and respected by his councillors. He was dark of complexion, with very white teeth and eyes like lightning, flashing when he was angry. He had strong arms and beautiful legs that you could write about. Those who had been with him in the past said he was a man whose handsome looks could outclass the men of other nations because of his striking stature; but when he was at home, this was not obvious.

H-e-e! The strong man – he was still a young man – started with the verdict and addressed Wele, the plaintiff, "Listen, Vuyisile's son. It's already a few days since senior men of my household left home on account of you, because you came to ask for an investigation into a sensitive issue relating to your homestead, but now the matter has become the whole nation's; it's still being investigated, hence it is taking so many days. You first went to Lucangwana, your headman, and Lucangwana gave his opinion, which has not been disputed by this court. Yes, although this court has already also heard from Nqabarha, we do not disagree with Lucangwana's opinion.

"Your people, who are this court, say, 'Go home, and look after the calf that you were looking after, protect Vuyisile's family, and come and report anything wrong that you see there at your home.'"

Wele stood up, giving praise, and went to kiss the King's foot, and came back to sit again in another place. Now the King turned to Babini: "Do you hear, Vuyisile's elder son? Did you hear the various arguments in this court relating to both of you? Did you hear the words put upon your younger brother by this court? Go home then, and work together with him in looking after your family and livestock, and help him in looking at whatever needs to be looked after, and we will see you together here at the Great Place; be obedient to him, and listen to him."

After the King had finished saying these words, he sat down, and covered himself with his kaross made from the skin of the leopard of the rocks. Babini and his uncle stood up and changed positions.

Phekesa, one of Babini's uncles, stood up, wanting to know if today the elder twin in this house of Phalo had changed status to be the younger one. Mbali answered, "Nothing like that was done." Phekesa was fuming: "Then what did I hear?" Mbali said, "You heard well, because the communication was clear."

The plaintiff and his company were seen taking their sticks, turning to go home, and so were the defendant and his companions.

There near the kraal, women were heard criticising everything bitterly while others ululated. Men were seen going to fetch their riding-oxen, while another fetched his stick in order to think about walking home. Smokers were seen lighting their pipes and smoking; others simply stood in the smoke, others squatted, and others were on their knees with somebody lighting their pipes for them. People were simply standing around. Some were muttering and disapproved of the verdict, criticising, pointing out incorrect conclusions. But the majority were impressed by how well the case had been argued, with all its corners being looked at, and at how skilfully the verdict was delivered.

While this turmoil prevailed, Dumisani, a praise singer who was Zolile's son, was heard saying,

Hoyina! Attention please! Hoyina!
Go home, all you people, the lawsuit has finished;
Go home, all you people; what was talked about is finished.
So says Zanzolo,
So says One-who-forces-his-way-through-scrub-of-forests, the
    one of Gcaleka,
The calves of the old cow –
Should they sleep on the road, you must know there is trouble.
So says the bull whom they praise for goring before it gores;
What would they say the day it judges?
Because it would announce its judgement by a double-barrelled
    whistle with a deep, rough sound if I watch!
Listen, all you people, let us give you the fullness of the heart,

Listen, all you people, let us tell you a tale:
Long, long ago, the day that mountains appeared,
One person was installed to rule over others.
It was said that person must be named, a person of royal blood,
It was said that person must be called the calf of the nation,
It was said that person must be obeyed by the community;
And he would then obey Qamata;
From whom laws and regulations will come;
When they are disobeyed, there will be disorder,
There will be turmoil and arguments among people,
It will be chaos and there will be madness in the land.
Those who grumble never perish,
Those who complain are still born even today.
They are standing on their bellies, and walk with the aid
    of a stick.
They are not pretending, they are created like that;
As we are correcting things, they are disturbing them:
Should we allow them, the whole nation would perish.
I say it easily, because they know that.
Fools have already blurted out foolish things,
They said that the bull was at Nqabarha.
This house of Xhosa, today, I'm done with it;
I'm done with it, as it confuses even the indigenous people,
So how will it be to the newcomers?
The leopard-with-knees of Khala has spoken,
The one whose eyebrows they look at, saying he's angry,
    has spoken,
The bull whose goring they hail even before he has gored.
There is just one little wound today, it's Lucangwana's.
You can go, my nation, the lawsuit of the twins has finished.
Go home, Sorharhobe has answered!
Ncincilili – *There I leave it!*

9

The aftermath of the case

When the praise singer of the Mpehle clan performed like that, the people fell silent, as he was a man whose words reverberated profoundly. When he said that that day, it cut deeply; people felt as if they had heard it for the first time, and their hearts were suddenly softened. Men sobbed whilst responding to the praises. While he was praising, food burnt in the pots in the presence of the women. None of the men at the Great Place felt like leaving; one who was smoking accidentally broke his pipe; some stood up naked, not even aware of it, and they were taken by surprise at how the seams of their blankets were unravelling, unravelling, and unravelling.

Those who knew this praise singer said that fortunately he had stopped soon enough, and did nothing devastating that day; they said if he had continued, people would have been injured. But indeed, people were already confirming that a few men had suffered injuries. The praise singer was a tall, well-built man, and he was used to the people as he had grown up among them. He carried two shields in the left hand and a short black stick in the right, and his style of feigning while performing was impressive: when he feigned beating down one man, he would pretend to fall on another, while beating down yet another with his stick.

A certain woman, Phikisani's wife of the Zangwa clan, was carrying a piece of firewood to add to a fire, but then she beat

Zamani's wife of the Ntlotshane clan with it, shoving it underneath her ncebetha, her apron. Another woman got bitten on the chin. Among the men the same happened. Everything went wrong: dogs fought, men shoved Ntsema of the Qadi clan into the thorn-branch kraal fence, and then the dogs bit him, and people started to intervene strongly from every side.

Phaki, a young man from the Vundla clan, was mentally not all there, but used to visit the Great Place and gatherings elsewhere which he treated as times for singing and dancing. He tied the calfskin he was wearing hastily, and began to sing and dance. When he was fighting someone with his stick, he got too close to the fire, and fell with his head right in the fire. Since his animal hide was loose, it fell down to his legs, and tied him so that he could not get up fast enough. It was impossible to save him; and so it happened that he could not answer or be called any more, and he died in the evening of that same day.

Trouble arose with Ndlombose as well. When Dumisani, the praise singer, mentioned fools, Ndlombose assumed that he was talking about Bhukwana, his younger brother. He asked Bhukwana if he could hear for himself now that Dumisani's praise singing was referring to him: "Do you realise that the name of the Langeni will from now on be viewed with contempt by other people?" The councillors had to intervene, calming the furious man down.

Nophaka was a girl from the Ncotshwa clan who was also a bit slow, and not good at speaking. She was present at the Great Place as well and people teased her, referring to her as Phaki's wife. She loved Phaki very much, but Phaki had wanted to stab anyone who talked about Nophaka's love for him; he did not want anything to do with her at all, claiming that she was just dumb. So when Phaki fell into the fire, this girl from the Ncotsho clan began to yell hysterically and was inconsolable, crying bitterly and blaming the praise singer, saying he was the one who had misled Phaki and led him to the place where the fire was. That was just one of many events that day.

Mfithi, an old man from the Kwayi clan, who had gone blind and deaf in his old age, lived at the Great Place. When he faintly heard all these noises around him, he immediately concluded that there was a war; that the nation had been driven out by the enemy, and that he, too, would be burnt in his home. He was spotted running out of his hut as fast as his decrepit legs could carry him. Without really getting anywhere, he lifted his hands into the air, shouting, "Forgive me Nation-greater-than-my-nation! I, your pauper, I am nothing." His daughter, Boniwe, rushed to him, calmed him down, and when the pressure subsided, he was taken back to his house.

Boys were gathering in groups below the homestead. One boy, Njeza, claimed that his father also knew how to praise-sing as he was always singing praises at home. Another boy, Ntlanganiso, said, "You are lying, young boy, since when does your father know how to sing praises?" When Njeza was still saying, "I am not lying, young..." Ndaba was already there, hitting Njeza with a stick, saying, "I don't like a lying boy!" Now the boys took it personally, and quickly split into groups; the other people there just heard the commotion below the homestead. Bystanders saw how Gonyela, a young man, son of Nyaba of the Jwarha clan, ran flat out to intervene, but fell into old pits near the homestead. One moment he was running, the next he felt himself tumbling down into these pits, face first. When the boys saw him, they said, "Good! It's our ancestors watching over us!"

Gonyela tried to stand up in the pits but kept slipping. At last people came to rescue him, but the young man could now do nothing as his leg was broken at the thigh, near the hip joint. He was carried out and taken to Gxuluwe, a traditional healer from the Ntakwenda clan, and the young man could walk again within a few days. But he kept wishing that those boys could experience what he had gone through, and, like many others, he also blamed the praise singer, saying that he did not know what had inspired all these iimbongi, these praise poets, who wanted to make a noise all the time. For good measure, he accused the twins too – if they had not quarrelled, he would not have been injured.

This was the chaos following the praise-singing by Zolile's son, Dumisani. When he had finished, he returned to his home. Slowly the rest of the men began to disperse in the direction of their homes, all the while analysing the details of the lawsuit.

Until then, the Xhosa had regarded the twin born first as the heir, and it was totally unheard of that it could change as it had on that day. Yes, and as you can imagine, there were those who claimed that the verdict indicated that from that case onwards, the twin born first was for ever to be regarded as the younger, and the elder was the one born last. I am really not sure what made them say this; they were not talking the truth.

10

Babini's conversion

When the verdict was given, everyone's attention was on Babini, because people thought that he would be so blinded by anger that he would resort to doing something rash. But Babini did not; he carried himself like a man.

When he was leaving the courtyard, he, like all the other men, took his stick and put it on his shoulder. He took out his pipe, and his uncle, Phekesa, lit it for him; he smoked, and they left. Everyone could see that Phekesa was furious. But Babini walked like a mild man, as if the matter was not weighing him down. The third man was a person who did not speak much: Lalo, Phekesa's younger brother, also an uncle of the twins.

When they left the Great Place, they came to the parting of the roads, the one going to Phekesa's home and the other to Vuyisile's home. Babini took the one going home. "Where are you going?" Phekesa asked angrily. Babini replied, "I am going home."

Phekesa: "To which home? Do you *have* a home? Are you going to that witch, your mother? What's wrong with you?"

Babini: "Nothing, I am going home."

Phekesa: "Do you hear, Lalo! Do you hear what he says? Do you see that she finished him, that witch, his mother? Let us leave him, let us leave him."

This angered Babini: "Uncle, my mother is not a witch; if there is witchcraft in all of this, it is between you and me."

He looked as if he could attack Phekesa, but Lalo intervened and they went their own way. Phekesa remained furious, "After making this vagrant a human being among other people, he rewards me by insulting me. Is it not because of *his* behaviour that Vuyisile's household was not cleansed, and is he not the one who unceremoniously chased me away? He takes after his mother!"

Babini walked straight home. When he arrived there, he passed the house to go and look at the cattle in the veld; he brought them to the kraal without any hitches, cleaned his hands and milked the cows, as if nothing in the world had happened.

At sunset it was time to eat. The mat for the serving of food was placed between the twins, with the maternal uncle, Mgqaliso, and a few other men present. All the men conversed as usual, as if nothing significant had just happened.

The following day at dawn, Babini took an axe, and chopped some branches with which he, assisted by Wele, closed a few of the openings in the kraal and fence. They spent the whole of that day together, until they eventually went together to fetch the cattle at sunset.

People who came to visit Wele about certain issues could not mention them in front of Babini. Those who wanted to discuss their matters with Babini did not mention them in front of Wele. That became a problem for the people, but not for the twins.

On the tenth day after the case, as the sun was setting, women were heard singing loudly at the homestead of Zuzani, the son of Mthana of the Kwayi clan. On that day, during this singing, Babini went to sleep, though some men came specially to fetch him, saying:

UNxange' engxangxasini –
You who stand and wait at the waterfall,

You who stop the wives of the ground hornbill,
You have lost the tune.
You all delivered it in a manly fashion
A song that should be sung in female fashion.
Do you see the homesteads of this river?
Their dancing when the waterfall sings for them?
Dove in front,
Duiker at the back,
The rope and the bucket boy from the Nzothwa clan.

Indeed, on this day "Ngxangxengxa" or He-who-stands-and-waits – Babini – did not entertain them at all; he let them know he was feeling lazy, and that was that.

The men left, analysing the behaviour of "Ngxangxengxa" – the name means one who is too lazy to go to the ceremony of the traditional transition rite of a girl who is to be initiated into young womanhood.

Vububi said, "Babini is acting like this because of that young conceited twin brother from his homestead."

Gqirhana said, "Yes, that's absolutely true, my men, this has affected him; do you know that we haven't seen him at a dancing ceremony at all since the verdict?"

Jongisa said, "That's absolutely true, and this will have an impact. Ngxanga... – Babini – is indeed milking at his home, goes out with the cattle, and comes back with them. He was also seen fencing the kraal the other day."

The festivities at Zuzani's homestead took days, with Babini seemingly not concerned. On the day of singing and dancing, he attended like all the other men; he danced and danced like all the dancers, until it came to an end, then went home with Wele.

One day there was an imbizo at the Great Place and, as usual, all the men went there. At sunset when the gathering dispersed,

Babini was called by the queen, the mother of the boy Sarhili. Sarhili was Hintsa's son and the future king, and was known as Zothana at the time. Sarhili's mother's name was Nomsa, and she was the daughter of Gambushe, the chief of the Bomvana. She ordered Babini, "Take that axe my child, and chop wood for your fathers!"

Babini immediately took off his blanket, picked up the axe, chopped wood, then made a fire, fetched water, cooked, and all of that. The sun set, then dawn came, but he continued with his chores, being an active man at this homestead amongst the women, a very handsome one with a headpiece consisting of one plain copper ring, and one whose trousers fitted exceptionally well.

On the fifth day at sunset, the King selected a big reddish cow and gave it to Babini, and then this son of Vuyisile left for home, stopping along the way, and reaching it by the evening.

From then on, Babini became a frequent visitor at the Royal House. Time and again he was called to do something there, and afterwards went home driving a cow. Clearly, the King liked him very much. "He's a young man who listens," and the women agreed. "He's not conceited, picking and choosing, but works for everybody in the same manner." The councillors said, "He's a strong man," and the milking men said, "He gives."

One day, a sparkling, wild, black cow with white spots on the face that had been seized by the Qwathi people gave birth. When the men milking the cows were busy, she was licking her calf near the gate inside the kraal. It was obvious that she was very vigilant and aggressive, not wanting the boys to come near her.

At one point Babini looked up, and he saw the boy, Zothana, being crushed into the branches of the kraal enclosure by this cow, and crying hysterically. The cow was furious: she had tossed Zothana with her horns after lifting him with her snout, and threw him through the air. When he crashed into the branches, she gored him in the stomach, puncturing him with her horn. Babini ran and untangled the boy, but the place where the horn had struck the boy became a lump; even to this day it is said, "He is the one who fought with a lump on the stomach." Babini's courage had saved him, because the cow had been coming straight at him.

After Babini had so absolutely outshone himself at the Great Place that day, he was given that very cow. He used the opportunity to tame her so that she no longer presented any danger to people, and she was milked right through that month.

At this time, Lucangwana, the headman, had already deliberated over another case concerning Babini. This time, Babini had been charged by the women for not attending the intonjane – a ceremony marking a girl's first menstruation – of his own daughter, Nompunzi. Moreover, he had not done his duties when the girl was secluded in the house, as tradition required. His sisters sided with the women on this matter, saying that if a woman had sidestepped her duty in this way, she would have been given a bad name by the other women.

The case was weighed up, and Babini was found guilty and fined a cow; it was slaughtered at the headman's place, and it was eaten by the men. Lucangwana took this opportunity also to make it clear that if a young man fell out of love with a girl for no good reason, he should make it known, so that other young people would know about it; and if he had a reason for rejecting a girl, he should also announce it and not just leave the girl guessing. The same applied to girls.

11

The cleansing of the homestead

The reader might like to know what happened between the twins and their uncle, Phekesa.

Let me start by saying that, right at the beginning of the lawsuit, Babini was not living at the family homestead, but was staying with his uncle, Phekesa. It was rumoured that Wele was influenced by his mother to lay a charge against Babini, and that she hated him; therefore it was assumed that if Babini was to go near his mother, she would bewitch him. In any case, even a headache at that time was regarded suspiciously, as if it was a bewitched headache. This was how things stood before the trial started.

But actually, Babini was quite aware that his mother was innocent; the culprit in all of this was none other than Babini himself. And according to him, the other offenders were his uncles, particularly Phekesa, for not reprimanding him, and not pointing out the things he did wrong at home, especially as Phekesa knew that he was a drifter. In the back of his mind, Babini always wondered why his uncle had simply dropped the issue after he, Babini, had chased him away the day he wanted to cleanse the household. Why had this matter ended up in thin air? Why had the uncle never referred to or discussed it again? If dealing with Babini's behaviour was beyond his rank and stature, why did the uncle not make an effort to gather the clans, so that he, Babini, could be properly reprimanded?

These things were quite clear to Babini, that is why he said to his uncle on the day of the verdict, "Mother is not a witch; if there is witchcraft in this, it is with you and me." Why was our uncle clinging to *me*, Babini wondered, whereas Wele was also here, the one who had the attitude of an adult person? When Babini arrived at those thoughts about his uncle, many truths were revealed to him, and it felt to him as if he, Babini, had been killing Vuyisile's homestead instead of supporting it.

H-e-e! The twins gathered with their mother, and they agreed that the homestead should be cleansed. The matter was then referred to their uncle, Phekesa, Gqabi's son of the Nzothwa clan; also to Geju, another close relative, as well as to the Mpandla clan of their mother's family, and the date was decided upon.

When the day arrived, Phekesa, who should traditionally have been the master of the ceremony of the ritual, was not there; instead he sent his younger brother, Lalo, to officiate in his place. He said he was visiting his daughter's home where there was an illness that had been brought to his attention by the Nyathi people.

The animal used for the ceremony was taken from the household: a black-and-white cow with impressive horns spreading like wings. But every morning during the times when aspects of the ceremony were being planned, the moment the kraal was opened, the chosen cow would go and stand right in front of Babini and Wele's homestead and bellow, then the other cattle would join her, and when they came back in the afternoon, she did the same thing before entering the kraal.

This was a great big animal that threw her horns back like a bushbuck, as if fighting. It seemed that the cow was taking over this place; they had not thought about it before and had to select another one.

Gunguluza, the animal that runs zigzag,
An old cow with bare, hairless patches on the body, is on
    her feet;
The cow that carries horns on her back
As she knows the law.
She goes to the Nzolo and the Nyelenzi clans
In the realm of the spirits.

Lalo, a very meek person, conducted the ceremony between the men and the dignitaries. The headman, Lucangwana, was among those who spoke, as did Mbiko Qalo of the Mfene clan of the Thembu tribe, and Gama Shiqi of the Khwemte clan, and Fuzile Nzuzo of the Kwayi clan, and other councillors.

The words were directed at Wele as head of the homestead: "Here is the family, Vuyisile's son; it should not disintegrate whilst you are here. Look after the Mpandla daughter, who gave birth to you; she should not suffer because of the death of Golomi's son." Speakers also referred to her as Lawule's daughter, saying, "Yes, daughter of Lawule, the Xhosa say, 'The sun does not set without news.' A day such as this one gets spoken about. You know how these children were raised by their father; we say so, you having been dependent on him. But today you are no longer his dependant: what has happened made you older. Be on good terms with your sons and they with you."

The councillors continued in this vein, preaching co-operation between the brothers. They also raised the issue that a young man should be shown a wife to help with the household chores for their mother, who was too old for kindling fires and fetching water.

At this juncture, a small group of men arrived from the home of Lucangwana, the headman. Lucangwana's son, Zenze, had chosen for himself the youngest girl, Cishiwe, from the twins homestead. The news was relayed, ten cows arrived before the wedding and the girl was taken to Lucangwana's. The cow of showing-humbleness-and-sour-milk-drinking was slaughtered, and after that a wedding cow. The event lasted a few days, and King Hintsa was also there. When the bridal party came back, they came also driving ten cows; then when they went there, accompanying the bride, they took two oxen for the traditional dance that was accompanied by clapping hands.

After a few months, the twins negotiated with their own relatives about who was to take a wife. Wele was determined that his older brother should be first; whatever others suggested, he refused point-blank. Then a girl was chosen for Babini from the Jwarha clan: Nyaba's daughter, a sister of Gonyela, he who had broken his leg at the pits on the day of the verdict. The name of the girl was Noli. The ceremony was carried out in the right way, and the days were filled with Babini's dancing – indeed "Ngxangxengxa" wore the cheetah-skin kaross that he had been given at the Great Place.

Babini's bridal party came back driving five cows (in addition to the cow and calf of consent, those given as a gift to his in-laws) because the bride's father had said that that number given should not be excessive.

Things went very well after the Nzotho clan's home was cleansed. Indeed, life flowed smoothly, and co-operation, peace and happiness strengthened in the homestead.

12

Unity is above the law

Two years after the verdict was given, Wele received word from the Royal House that the King wanted to carry out the ceremony of consoling the homestead, ukukhuza. When the message came, Wele was surprised that it was sent to him instead of to his older brother, Babini.

He immediately gave his brother the message, and said that it was a mistake that the Royal House had sent it to him. This he said while the messengers from the King were still there.

Babini replied that the Royal House had not erred, as it was following the decision of the court. Wele disagreed and said, not at all, that was *not* what the court had ruled. The messengers from the Royal House interrupted, wanting to know from Wele what the verdict was. He said, "I say that this message should have been sent to my elder brother, this one." They repeatedly tried to determine the gist of the matter, until they decided to leave it like that. Wele asked whether the King had already determined a day for the ceremony, but there was no date in mind yet, as the King wanted to announce the matter first. Wele agreed that that was right.

The messengers were sent back with these words, "You should say to the honourable members of the Royal House, I am grateful for this decision; but before the ceremony proceeds, the word from the Royal House has to come in a clear manner."

The messengers left and relayed Wele's answer as it was given to them.

This answer led to a commotion at the Royal House. The King consulted his close councillors, interrogating what should be done. They discussed and re-discussed the whole verdict, and were split into two camps. Some said Wele was correct; the issue of comforting the bereaved could not be referred to him, not being the heir. Others said that Wele was the rightful heir, according to the law that had been deliberated here in the court of this Great Place.

This issue of the rightful heir again became the focus of another major discussion that rapidly spread to the entire nation. According to Babini, the ruling should not have been directed in his favour, because the case was interrogated and he was charged. He was charged with facts visible even to an infant. It became clear that the honourable King had no choice but to convene a large meeting at which those councillors involved in the original lawsuit were also required to be present.

Some were saying, "Where is Khulile then, our advisor on these twins." Others warned, "Khulile said that he should not be called for the issue of the twins." And others, "We said that there was no point in going to Nqabarha." Some were of the opinion that there would never be happiness until these twins were separated and scattered about, the one to be in one nation, and the other in another.

The invitations to the meeting were extensive, and Vuyisile's twins were called as well. The Royal House councillors flocked to sit in the courtyard as on previous occasions. The throne of the King was taken out and put in its place; then the King followed and the court sang his praises as a greeting.

On this day a man from the Ngwevu clan, Bangiwe, son of Mjonga, stood up and said, "Yes, councillors, you should not be weary of a matter which is yours. No one has ever tired of correcting things at his home. The reason for this meeting is the continuing confusion in regard to the law. Word came from this home to Vuyisile's homestead, saying that they wanted to perform the ceremony for consoling a family. Then a difference of opinion erupted: this one said he is the younger, and that one said he is not an heir. Today you have been called to clarify this matter."

Ngxelo Gabisa of the Qocwa clan stood up and said, "How many times should this matter be clarified, my father? Am I mistaken if I say this place was full of people coming to clarify it only yesterday, and they decided on it, saying that they were now satisfied to leave it at that?"

Bangiwe answered, "Yes, child of my home, that is the truth in its entirety. But the issue regarding this family's consoling ceremony is: how should it be done?"

The court now was directed at the twins, in order to hear their opinion. Wele said that he had merely been stopping a branch that was about to fall upon Vuyisile's family. As the owner had been playing truant, but was now back, he, Wele, no longer knew who he was because this court had said clearly then that it does not overrule Lucangwana's verdict.

Babini said that he did not know whether this court should expect him to speak. He was simply obeying the summons that had been communicated to him in broad daylight from this place, but otherwise he had nothing to say.

Then the twins were asked to go home until they were called later. The men who remained behind discussed in detail the matter of the twins, revisiting every possible approach from all sides as to what had been said. They leaned heavily on Khulile's wisdom that "it is actions that make an heir, because, even the heir if he does not act, forfeits his heirdom". Also the wording within the verdict, "Do you hear, Vuyisile's elder son?" was interrogated

It was said that that utterance alone had unmistakably stated that Babini had not been demoted to being the younger son.

The discussion of the councillors ended there, and they dispersed. After a few days, the twins were called again to the Royal House. Many prominent men of the area were there. Again, the whole matter concerning the verdict on the twins was revived, and so was Khulile's speech, and the speech analysing the verdict on the previous day. The court completed its verdict by thanking Wele for all the actions he had undertaken to look after the family without a father, and for not fearing to refer this matter to the court to be resolved for him, so that his actions should remain clear. Mxhuma Matyeni said this on behalf of the honourable King.

The King completed the event by giving Wele a spear, and a well-built red cow with white spots on the face, that was still suckling her sturdy calf. Then he told him to go home, saying he was a man.

Vuyisile's sons went home, making all kinds of happy detours. And the people assured one another that co-operation and harmony were bigger than the law; it was indeed true that *unity is strength.*

13

Comforting the bereaved

After that month, the King sent Fuzile Thinga of the Qadi clan and Mdunywa Hela of the Nyele clan to Vuyisile's homestead to tell the people that the King was coming the following month, at full moon, to console Vuyisile's family.

When these men were walking past the houses, they were asked where they were from and where they were going. They talked but did not mention their purpose. Some said, "We can see that you are going to those twins. They are troublesome, but what is surprising is that the Royal House loves them so much; because we see them frequently driving cattle, coming from the direction of the Royal House."

The men continued and did not respond to these words. Eventually, before sunset, they reached the place they had been sent to, and they were given a place, properly prepared, to stay in and sleep in. They were questioned about the news that they had brought from the Royal House, and they said what had to be said. This time the notice was directed at Babini, as the heir of this homestead; and so the announcement was welcomed, and the time that had been decided upon suited the household.

The following day, the messengers went home at midday When they arrived back at the Royal House, they reported what they had seen and heard. As they were talking about various things, they mentioned that Babini had a boy who was already walking, by his wife, Nyaba's daughter of the Jwarha clan. It so happened that the Royal House heard about that. Two men were sent to Babini to take a fine from him in the form of a cow, for not having reported the birth of the child.

Babini tried to explain that he *was* going to report the child, but it did not help. He then said that he had reported this matter to the wives when he recently went to the Royal House. But that did not help either, the men saying, "We are not sent to discuss a case, we are here to drive back a fine." Eventually he took out an ox of even colour with a white back, a calf of the very cow he had been given by the Royal House, coming from the Qwathi clans.

When this ox was leaving, his mother said, "We old women are not listened to. How long have I spoken about this? Mistakenly, I thought it had been done by now." Babini apologised, indicating that this matter had been overlooked by him and Wele, although they often talked about it here at home.

The young men drove this ox and left it at the household of Ntshizi Langa of the Zimeni clan, from the Thembu tribe, a man who was a representative of the Royal House. This was because the ox could not go to the King, as it was coming from a homestead that had not yet been consoled in accordance with Xhosa law. The councillors called one another in order to eat the fine, although, as it turned out, another old cow was slaughtered instead of this ox, as he was regarded as being an animal of superior breeding.

The time approached for the King to go to Vuyisile's homestead, and the day was set. By now the wise old cow was already presenting herself:

Gunguluza, the animal that runs zigzag,
An old cow with bare, hairless patches on the body, is on her feet;

The cow that carries horns on her back
As she knows the law.
She goes to the Nzolo and the Nyelenzi clans
In the realm of the spirits.

This cow did not have many tricks, but in the afternoons, she would come back alone from the veld and stand in the courtyard, doing nothing. Then in the morning at sunrise, she would stand near the gate looking at the door of the main homestead, take two or three mouthfuls, and then leave, with her horns that flowed from her head along her back, like those of a bushbuck.

A day before the prescribed day of the ceremony, hordes of people were seen going to Vuyisile's homestead in Thoboshane. Some slept over with friends living nearby, and some slept in the courtyard with their riding-oxen until sunrise, their arrival at the homestead not seen by anybody.

The King arrived at dusk on the day preceding the ceremony, and he came with a large group of councillors. When he arrived, the cow, Gunguluza, was unexpectedly standing at the gate without having been driven there. It thus became obvious that the ritual should be started on that very day. As was the tradition, Gunguluza was presented with a few words, then lassoed with a rope, forced down, stabbed in the belly and, as was customary, the aorta was pulled; she bellowed a few times, "B-h-o-h-o-h-o-h-o-!" A chilling sensation and a shudder ran down the spines of even those inside the house; she died, and was then slaughtered. The sun set to prepare for the next day.

When the sun was about to leave the mountains, people were already moving about like white ants. Dishes with amasi, sour milk, stood in a row; there was chopping of meat in preparation for the meal; and there was no end to the pots of food, some going to the kraal and others behind the kraal to the women.

After eating, Mborhoma of the amaBamba clan stood up and said, "Attention, people of this kraal! I am compelled by law. It is said the time has come, the law must proceed, and the noise must end!"

At that moment it became quiet, pipes were put down, the Nzothwa household went to their place, and breastfeeding women covered their nipples.

First Mvaba Gxekiso of the Cirha clan stood up, saying "Excuse me, Nzothwa clan! Excuse me, Mpandla clan, as well! I am nobody; I prepare the road, because today our King, Khawuta's son, will be walking on it. The word that he will say to you, Vuyisile's son, is an old word, we were born under the same word; and the next generation will also hear it. These many people have come to hear that word, so that in future they will be witnesses, confirming that Khawuta's son spoke to you, he spoke to your mother too, and he spoke to the Nzothwa clan as well. I am stopping there; it seems as if I have already said too much."

Luhadi Khongo of the Dala clan stood up and said, "Oh, yes, councillors, it is good you are here, it's good you are doing this, as you are here to soothe the wound of this family. People are people by consoling each other; it is only the dog that soothes itself. This is an old homestead; when the place was not so populated, when Phalo's nations were still few, this homestead was already in existence. With these words, I am saying, listen. Today your King will present an old law at this homestead; he will come to mine tomorrow, and come to yours the next day, and we will be at his the following day."

Mxhuma Matyeni of the Mkhomazi-Qhinebe clans stood up and said, "Deep talking has been done today with the Nzothwa family, and not with us. We also include you, the Mpandla family; because you were included the day Lawule's daughter, the mother of the twins, walked into this, Vuyisile's courtyard.

We have come to say that you should see each other, and know that you are related, Gomomo's family; Gqabi and Golomi are not from other families, they sprang from the same hip of their father. When we say that, Phekesa, uncle of the twins and Gqabi's son, we say that we commission this family to you, as you see that Babini is a child. During his childhood, he was still looked after; when he was reprimanded by this court the other day, you were there, but his behaviour had elicited no response from you. You too, Lawule's daughter, as everyone is sitting here and saying this and that, the King and the people are here to take you away from the place of the owls, the place of people of lower status, so that from today you are a homeowner, as you were before. People must visit this household, it should not be deserted. Please look after Nyaba's child, and teach her how to be a wife, and tell her that being a wife means looking after the destitute. You, Babini, look after your father's child, Wele, and never despise his previous attempts to make you a better person. Look after Lawule's daughter, who has been looking after this homestead for all these years. Look after Khawuta's son; when you see him feeling out of place when he arrives at your home, it is because he is thinking about the old people of this homestead, of your home, of the Nzothwa clan."

The Ntshezi Langa, the King's right-hand man, of the Zima clan, stood up and spoke to the family: "A lot has been said, and you may have many responsibilities, but the true and helpful directives will be those coming from within you. Therefore we are saying, 'Our condolences,' the King has come to say that to you, these councillors have come to say that too. Let there be peace; things will be fine as of today, Gomomo's family, and you can come out of the forest of mourning. It was like this for the elders, and it will also be like this for the following generations. We have not come to reopen the scab of your wound, instead we have come to hea you; yes, this event, this death, took place a long time ago, and putting right the small matters around it through law was nearly forgotten. You have already stepped where you should not have gone; but the problem is not with you, it is this dispersal, this scattering of us all. Today we curtail that evil. We are directing these words at you, Babini, you, the heir of this family. Look after it, so that it does not disintegrate; and look after yourself, and do not allow bad habits to come back to you; and look after Lawule's daughter, your mother, so that she does not differ from others; and look after your King, Khawuta's son."

At last the King stood up: "Let the ears not clash in confusion, Gcaleka's people. The councillors who have spoken directed this at Babini, Vuyisile's older son. They have finished; there are no other words left. I am standing and speaking, because I bear the name of the King of this nation – Phalo. So say the people of your home, Babini. Things will only be right when they say what you also say; if you do not say the same, nothing will come of it."

"We have come to comfort you; we have come to console you. We say nothing new has happened; it has been there since our beginnings, since our origins. Go among the people as of today, and be no longer laughed at by birds; go to the Great Place as well and never despise your younger brother, Wele, and Lawule's daughter; they should always be uppermost in your mind."

The meeting dispersed after these words, and people went home.

14

The death of Khulile, and Nompumza's history

When the King arrived home from the ritual of comforting the bereaved, there were three men from Nqabarha who had come to announce that the old sage, Khulile, had died.

But before we get to the details of the dying Khulile's final instructions, and the value of his vision for the nation, we will move back a little, and first tell the story of Nompumza of the Zotsho clan.

Before the lawsuit of the twins, a man from a different group had arrived with a cluster of subordinates. One could see that he was not just any man, but a man with status, a reputation, among his people. When asked where he came from, he said he was from UMzimkhulu, and that he was looking for animals to hunt; he said that his people were the Zotsho, and his name, Nompumza.

As it happened, Nompumza was not telling the truth when he said he was looking for animals. He was an expert thief with followers ruling various groups of thieves.

He, in turn, had been sent by his chief from the north to come to this place. Their people there had heard that among the Xhosa people who have died wake and return. This news stunned the group in the north; for them it was not a small issue, and it spread. So the chief of the north was looking for a reliable person with wisdom, cunning, and strength to go and investigate the issue of resurrection of the dead.

Then the chief found Nompumza. The Zotsho people of long ago were related to the Nguni people on the western side and the eMbo people on the eastern side; therefore the Zotsho are people who have always been among these nations, to this day.

When the chief found Nompumza, a man who knew many places and many nations, he called him and sent him to the south, saying, "Go and investigate this thing for us; we hear that dead people rise from death among the Xhosa people."

At last Nompumza arrived among the Xhosa, but he did not come across the resurrection. He even went to the house of the Right Hand of the Rharhabe tribe; but no, he did not see it. He arrived in a beautiful, happy land, with all its delights and pleasures, but he did not hear anybody talking about any dead person who had been resurrected.

Eventually he returned home and reported that there was no such thing; there was no resurrection of the dead. But his chief did not believe this, and he told him to go back to the south. To accompany him, he provided him with men whom he could rely on.

So Nompumza made a second journey to investigate the "rising of the dead", and this time too, it was without success. But instead of going back, he chose to remain in Ndlambe's area, and abandoned his thoughts of going home. He ended up being a resident in Ndlambe's country, at Gqunube and at Kwelerha.

Nompumza now entered fully into all the pleasures of the Ndlambe group. Because he was a singer, he was taken by Nxele of the Cwerha clan, a wealthy man known all over the Ndlambe nation, who always had Nompumza leading the song, iThabu, in the Nkanga forests near Gompo – the current East London. But as time went by, Nompumza felt homesick and asked to return home, but his master, Nxele, did not want to allow it, and said, "Your land is in a bad state back at home, it's just disintegrating." Nxele was telling the truth, because it was the time of Shaka's turmoil.

The man from the north stayed there permanently, and he married one of the Ndlambe girls. The elders of Ndlambe did not like seeing Nompumza, a man from elsewhere, being so elevated: indeed, when Nompumza married, he was given cattle from an ancestral herd with which to pay lobola, and not from izizi, the chief's pool of cattle that had been confiscated from people whom diviners had smelt out for wrongdoing.

At last the elders of Ndlambe gave Nompumza his own place, a fact that he hid from his former masters in the north. And so the hero from the north remained with the Ndlambe, not going back to his chief to report on "the rising of the dead". Even today, Nompumza's offspring can be found at Rhabhula. They have not returned to the north to give a report on the resurrection.

In this account of Nompumza, I have tried to make connections and give insight into the visions and the last words of the old sage Khulile that follow in this story. At the time, the meaning of his words seemed quite hazy.

The reader might assume that Khulile's death – and the words he spoke before it – coincided with Ntsikana's[11] first visions in Rharhabe's land.

I was saying earlier that when the King arrived home from the ceremony of comforting the bereaved at the twins' homestead there were three men who had come to announce that Khulile was dead. These men were Galada Sobi of the Zangwa clan, Dileka Fusini of the Qocwa clan, and Moyikwa Sidumbi of the Qwambi clan. They were accompanied by a young man, Vula from the Vundla clan.

In short, these men arrived and said that they had been sent to announce the death of Khulile. Before he left this world, Khulile had held large gatherings and meetings for about a month, but he was not ill. He gave his last instructions to his whole family, and divided his belongings among them. He then went to the Royal House, and announced that he had about one month left on this earth.

Khulile had said, "The first point is this: people must discard witchcraft. There are good times ahead, but sad ones are also coming. Good times are coming, but also times of sorrow. A man will come from the land of Rharhabe who will talk about life's great issues; but if what he says is not heeded, that will be the death of the nation.

"The second point: the topic that Nompumza talked about is the truth: the resurrection of the dead. In order for it to be clear, it will be seen through a Book, a Volume with many parts gathered into it, that will come from the west, carried by foreign nations emerging from the sea. You have to scrutinise this Book, as the rise and fall of nations depends on it.

"The third point: in time to come, many will say that the speech of a girl[12] destroyed the nation and the whole tribe, because all the cattle will die, even people will perish in the veld, and a foul smell will blanket the land. That will not be destruction; it will be a sacrifice made for the Book that will come. The girl will not say what she wants to say, she will say what she is instructed to say. You should not cry, because those things will pass with the passage of time.

"The fourth point: this is to do with the time of darkness, or the time of pandemonium. That time will be like the darkness that precedes dawn; that time is the darkest, it becomes very, very dark, and yet when that darkness fades away it will already be dawn. In that time, discord and children's disobedience will grow; the nation will be destroyed and will be under the rule of unknown, foreign and harsh nations. The chieftaincy will become powerless; it will die out, and will simply be something talked about. By that time people will not know where they come from, and where they are going; darkness and chaos will reign.

"But do not lose hope and give up on yourselves, although some will already be selling their children; but you must look to the Book, study it in the morning and in the evening, because help will come through greater understanding.

"The fifth point: during that time of darkness there will be a great war like no other war in size. But it will not come to you directly; it will be between foreign nations, but because they rule you, it will affect you, although it will only come to you in passing. After that war, if you look at the Book, you will get some grasp, some understanding of humanity and human kindness. But what I am preaching above all is that within this pandemonium of nations and tribes, and this abusive behaviour, you should look after one another, and know one another, and become one. Never abandon your chiefs."

So said the men from Nqabarha; and they ended by saying, "The old man said this speech should be delivered here at his home."

The men from Nqabarha spent three days at the Great Place, and left after they and the chief's son who had sent them had been thanked. They were asked to convey the King's shock at hearing that Khulile, one of the nation's great fathers, had died.

15

The arrival of tribes

Three months after the men who announced Khulile's death had left, another three men arrived from Nqabarha and from over at Shixini village, in Chief Somlilo's jurisdiction. When they were asked where they came from, they said they had been sent by the chief to inform the Great Place that there was a black tribe that had come to them, who were very thin because of their poverty and their state of disintegration.

When asked the name of that tribe, the messengers explained that they had not clearly worked out who they were, although they looked like Nompumza from the north, and they also spoke like him. Other questions were also asked about the tribe, and they answered them satisfactorily. After the councillors had expressed their gratitude, the King instructed them: "Please look after those newly arrived people; they belong to us, and to you as well. Give them food, and give them clothes to wear, and treat them with kindness so that they feel that you are not the tribe that destroyed them; please do not take them lightly or just play with them."

Quite some time after Somlilo's messengers had left, five men arrived from the small homestead of the Royal House in Ndlambe's jurisdiction at Mnyameni. There were delighted expressions of pleasure and happiness when they arrived, because Ndlambe was very much loved at his home in the land of Gcaleka.

These men had been sent by Ndlambe to announce Nxele[13]. At that time, Nxele was strongly against witchcraft and divination. When the messengers were announcing Nxele, they also announced another thing, although they were told that they should present it in a news-like manner.

They said that there was a tribe coming from the west. They were white in colour and their hair was very smooth and reddish.

When they were asked questions about this tribe, the messengers could not answer them satisfactorily, because they had just heard about this tribe, and had not seen them for themselves. The Great Place councillors expressed their gratitude to the messengers and the King said: "Yes, children of my home, I am grateful that you continue to make me a person, by telling me about events that happen. You then will have wisdom; if it is a tribe that comes through disintegration, take hold of them and make them forget about their disintegration. If it is a strong tribe, retreat first, and understand which things make them powerful, and study them. You must not run away from them, and only stop trouble if it is an angry nation."

Two years after Ndlambe's messengers announcing Nxele had left, some powerful men who had been sent by Chief Ngqika (the fourth among them being a young man), arrived at Hintsa's Great Place. When they were interrogated, the messengers confirmed that it was Ngqika, the son of Mlawu, who had sent them. He had asked them to announce Ntsikana, the son of Gabha. The messengers talked a lot about Ntsikana, his beginnings, his deeds, and his speeches.

The second thing that these men announced was that a white tribe had been seen. "It comes from the sea; it is a tribe that looks as though it regularly attacks other tribes. Their language is so complicated, no one understands it. As for fighting, they are powerful people who fight using the heavens; the heavens thunder once, smoke and fire explode, and then something falls in the distance."

The messengers from Ngqika talked a lot about various things. They were also told about the tribe that had come from Shixini, and that also became news.

The King ended the exchange by saying, "Tell my father's child there, Ngqika, that I'm just his dog; he should not tire of always acting like this, coming and reporting. About Ntsikana, tell him that 'actually the Creator of things is always there; we are mere dogs to him. He should work together with Ntsikana, lest there be blessings to us through that man, because he was sent from heaven to our home.' About the white tribe that is coming, he should be kind to them, until they see their inhumanity themselves. If they are wise people, obey and learn from them; he should not hasten to fight, until we hear from Qamata what to do."

Many people had accompanied Ngqika's councillors from Rharhabe's land, and there was singing and dancing and the joy of feeling happy. On their way home they slept at various places, and livestock was slaughtered for them.

A year passed by, and the messengers from Ndlambe came again; this time they were seven respected men. They said that they had been sent hastily, because they were coming with a very painful matter. A man from the Great Place responded with a serious "Hmmm…"

The messengers said that they had been sent by Chief Ndlambe, with the news that his son, Ngqika[14], had unexpectedly revolted against him and abducted his mother, Thuthula, to be by his side.[15] When the father tried to discuss this matter "on the hill", as the cases of chiefs were always deliberated there, it was of no help at all. That was why the father, Ndlambe, felt that he should immediately report it at the Great Place, which he saw as his home, and where help was to be found.

The reader might know that Ngqika had once imprisoned his father, Ndlambe, as well. He had even imprisoned Hintsa while Hintsa was still a boy.

Hearing this, Khawuta's son, King Hintsa, became emotional, and his penetrating eyes looked as if they would burst into flames, but he was as quiet as a rod, and said not a word. So the councillors of the Great Place recognised that this was true; things were really very bad.

In short (as I am not narrating the story of this war), about a month later, the army of the Gcaleka people was already over the Kei River, on its way to punish Ngqika for his misdeeds. Zanzolo, Hintsa himself, was also there, although the army was under the command of Vurhu, Khawuta's son from the smaller homestead of the Royal House.

That day the Hleke and Dange groups went home, and joined the side of Hintsa's Great Place, as did the Dushane group and the Gqunukhwebe group of Phatho, and by the time the sun set, they were in the valleys of Debe Nek.

I will not go into Ntsikana's words in detail. He spoke about how to try to prevent Ngqika from attacking. The army from the Great Place was very united, asking what strategy they should use to attack and overpower Ngqika. Ntsikana was still giving advice when Mnyaluza blew the whistle and commanded an attack. The Manxoyi and Ntsadu people, however, were asking, "When did this homestead start involving itself with diviners, with rain-makers? Pfff...!"

But indeed, Ngqika was defeated in the great battle of Amalinde. He was then told to move to the Meva region, but instead he went to summon help from white colonists, promising them the Ngqakayi region in return.

16

The praise poet

King Hintsa went back home after punishing Ngqika, not realising that Ngqika had then gone to fetch tribes to fight against him. Indeed, Ngqika returned from Thambo, near Khobonqaba where he had negotiated with the white tribe, and came back as a criminal. He then killed Ndlambe – it was only Ndlambe as King Hintsa had already left.

When the King and his army reached home, and while there was still confusion, with people standing about everywhere, Dumisani, Zolile's son, from the Mpehla clan, the praise poet of the Great Place, shouted:

Ho-o-o-o-o-yini! Ho-o-o-o-yini!
So I say, who carried it on my back!
So I say, who said he can talk!
I wonder what animal you said I was,
The one that could talk about not-talked-about things?
As of today the land is ill at ease;
As of today this earth is being bitten by pain;
You must be aware of what is in the stomach,
That which is in the womb, you must be aware of it;
Today it's as if something strange will be born;
It's as if an animal unknown by any hole will be born.
A-a-a-attention! A-a-attention!

The voice of the trumpet horn spoke, the day they left,

The horn of the cow rang out to assemble us,

The day we crossed this Kei River being so prepared;

The day Zanzolo stood up without a word,

We saw flames coming from his eyes,

We saw the spread of smoke through his nose,

We heard the sound of sharp whistles through our ears.

Today someone said the animal's hackles are rising,

The thing that they always said was there, was there today,

Because they looked at his eyebrows, and said he was angry;

Today those eyebrows mean clouds, see them thunder,

Today they make lightning; see there's no life for people.

Someone says today is today,

The land is upside down at the place of Rharhabe,

An unknown and evil deed has happened at the place of amaXhosa.

Awu! What can we say about earthly matters!

What was in the mind of the child, to go back to his mother's womb?

The blue cranes[16] stacked in heaps lying dead at Hoho;

Iron ate blood at Hoho;

Trees clashed against trees at Hoho;

The skin of the cow spoke at Hoho;

Beating and beating at Hoho;

A person passed, leaving no dying charge at Hoho;

He went to many others in the blink of an eye at Hoho;

The black vulture and its dogs ate at Hoho;

A large flock ate and left some for the white-necked raven at Hoho;

The hyena ate and gave some to the Cape hunting dog at Hoho;

The bluebottle fly ate and left some for the worms at Hoho;

Ho-yi-i-i-i-i-i-i-ni!

Please put down the weapons, young men;
Please put down the shields, hot-headed men;
Seemingly, according to Rharhabe you have succeeded,
Though when I look, it seems that there is a split.
You have to go now; so many things need to be rectified,
Because you did not ask anyone to look after your homes,
Yes, indeed, you left children burning each other.
It's one after the other, a row, a horde, a procession
So many other things you must go and fight –
Did you not hear of the vision of that old sage Khulile?
Did you not hear about things that are going to happen on
    this earth?
Did you not hear the great news of the coming Book?
Are we not going to ask you to look at it for us?
For our eyes are already with the white-necked raven.
Did you not hear about the man from the Right-hand
    homestead who's to speak?
He's been heard already by this group.
They call him the son of Gabha from the Cirha clan.
Did you not hear about the girl who will also speak?
It is said we will say it is destruction, whereas it is sacrifice.
Did you hear about the tribe with very smooth hair!
It is said they are people who play with lightning.
I, Zolile's son, say to you folk,
Go home and don't sleep, the land is reverberating –
I say that it will give birth to a monstrous creature;
It will give birth to an animal that no hole knows.
Go home and do not sleep, there come pools of blood;
Go home and do not sleep, there comes the end of humanity;
Go home and do not sleep, your fathers will sell you out;
Go home and do not sleep, you too will sell your fathers out;
Go home and do not sleep, chieftaincy will fade away;

Go home and do not sleep, you will look into the Book for us;

Go home and do not sleep, you will witness the shooting of the star;

Go home and do not sleep, you will look out for Zanzolo;

Go home and do not sleep, you are the base supporting the nation;

Go home and do not sleep, the families are in danger;

Go home and do not sleep, there comes a time of darkness;

Go home and do not sleep, we will not be here forever;

Go home and do not sleep, give service to the coming generation;

Go home and do not sleep, I say the real war has come.

When Dumisani was reciting those words, the honourable King Hintsa was so filled with emotion that he wept profusely. He said that that particular time of Darkness had become as clear as daylight to him, as if it had the brightness of a sun-ray; and those things had become real, as if they would happen during the days of his reign and that he should be grateful that, seemingly, he would be sacrificed for his father's nation, and die before the days of evil came. He spoke of that and cried inconsolably.

At that point, old men covered their heads and also cried loudly; and the young men could not endure that.

Women came in droves to meet the returning army, moving among and bumping into each other, singing and dancing. But at this moment of the King's crying, they could not contain themselves; they clutched their heads, and went around the homestead crying loudly.

The praise poet, too, was weeping copiously, and he threw himself down on his stomach, stabbed two spears deeply into the ground, and while clinging to them said, "My father! My father! My lord! My lord!"

From there people dispersed and went home, and it was all so bad, so sad, for everybody who was there. And all that the praise poet had spoken about was examined and reflected on by the whole nation.

Notes

1 The British King George V (Gogi) and his wife, the queen (Magogi).

2 In the Xhosa calendar, isiLimela is equivalent to June, and is named after the bright constellation of stars (the Pleiades) that appears then, and that is associated with the time for cultivation and planting of crops.

3 The court of King Hintsa, son of Khawuta.

4 A reference to the Xhosa tradition of using ochre, a type of red earth-based pigment, to colour clothing and parts of the body.

5 Babini's "two fathers" were brothers of his biological father, Vuyisile; in keeping with tradition, they were expected to be like fathers to their late brother's children.

6 Tshiwo was the father of Phalo, i.e. great-great-grandfather of Hintsa.

7 Mxhuma is referring to ukukhuza, a ceremony to comfort a bereaved family, conducted by a chief, usually a year after the head of a household has died. The purpose is to offer condolences and also to install the eldest son in the place of his father.

8 Majeke was one of Phalo's councillors. It is said that Phalo had arranged to marry a daughter of an Mpondo king and a daughter of a Thembu king. Unexpectedly, both bridal parties arrived on the same day. Choosing one woman to be the Great Wife might have offended the family of the other bride, and Majeke suggested making one the senior wife and the other the "wife of the Right Hand". This was accepted by Phalo, establishing a tradition. (J. Peires, *The House of Phalo*, 1981)

9 Inqilo, the Cape longclaw, a bird traditionally believed to be a sure sign of a safe and successful journey when it appears to a traveller.

10 A reference to ukulungiswa komzi, the ritual of "putting right" or cleansing the homestead, performed by a family after a death, especially the death of the father of the family.

11 Ntsikana (c. 1780–c. 1820) claimed to have mystical visions. He was rejected by Ndlambe, and attached himself to Ngqika, among the Rharhabe. Strongly influenced by Christianity, and a promoter of peace and submission, he wrote a hymn that is famous to this day.

12 A reference to Nongqawuse (c. 1841–1898), a young Xhosa woman whose prophecies led to the cattle-killing movement and famine of 1856–1857.

13 Nxele, also known as Makhanda, was regarded as a prophet and war-doctor to whom Ndlambe gave a home. He brought together Xhosa

chiefs, and led their armies against colonial forces, but was captured by the British. In 1819 he drowned, trying to escape from imprisonment on Robben Island.

14 Ndlambe had acted as regent for his young nephew, Ngqika, standing in for his father (Ndlambe's brother, Chief Mlawu) who had died when Ngqika was a child. Mqhayi refers to Ndlambe as Ngqika's father in the text, reflecting Xhosa tradition that a man's brothers were also fathers to his children.

15 Mqhayi's reference to this scandal in Xhosa history is very discreet. Thuthula was a young wife of Ndlambe (Ngqika's uncle/father), and therefore tradition dictated that Ngqika's relationship with her should have been that of a mother and son, not of lovers. Mqhayi refers to Thuthula as being Ngqika's mother. The abduction was regarded as incestuous and provoked outrage.

16 Feathers of the blue crane were awarded to Xhosa warriors for bravery, and they wore these in battle.

Glossary

Great Place the home of a chief or king; in this novel, the home of King Hintsa

headman a senior man responsible for a certain area, reporting to a chief

imbizo a gathering, a calling-together of people

imbongi (plural **iimbongi**) a traditional praise poet, who performs and recites a dramatic form of oral poetry that may include praises, historical allusions, and criticism

ingqithi the custom of cutting off the terminal joint of one of the fingers of a newly born child.

kaross cape or blanket made of animal skins stitched together

Mfecane a period of large-scale migrations of people in southern Africa, many of whom were fleeing from wars, especially at the time of Shaka

Ncincilili I'm done! (used to indicate that a poem or story is finished)

Qamata the supreme God of the Xhosa

Right-hand House the household that is second in importance in a chief's homestead; it is secondary to the home of the senior wife

Royal House the home of the king, where his senior wife lives, and where the heir is expected to be born. (Hintsa's Royal House is also referred to as the Great Place in Mqhayi's novel.)

sombre bulbul an olive-brown bird, common in forests in the eastern regions of southern Africa (recently renamed sombre greenbul)

About the translator

Thokozile Mabeqa

Thokozile Mabeqa was born in Alice in the Eastern Cape, in 1952. She is now retired but is still involved with academic work at the University of the Western Cape (UWC), where she has lectured on literature, cultural studies, translation, and editing both in English and isiXhosa. She has a Master's degree in translation studies from Stellenbosch University and another Master's degree in oral literature from the University of the Western Cape. She began her teaching career in the Eastern Cape, then she moved to Cape Town to pursue the same career. Later she lectured in methods of teaching isiXhosa and school management at a college of education in Cape Town. She has also taught first-time learners of isiXhosa in her private capacity. She was involved in developing a curriculum for isiXhosa communication at the Peninsula Technikon (now the Cape Peninsula University of Technology) before moving to UWC. Mabeqa has a wide range of translation experience, from academic texts to national government documents, and has also assisted the Stellenbosch University Language Centre.

To view the translators speaking about the Africa Pulse series, visit
www.youtube.com/oxfordsouthernafrica